TALES FROM THE
ODYSSEY
PART TWO

This volume includes:

BOOK FOUR
THE GRAY-EYED GODDESS

BOOK FIVE
RETURN TO ITHACA

BOOK SIX
THE FINAL BATTLE

TALES FROM THE

ODYSSEY

PART TWO

by MARY POPE OSBORNE

DISNEP · HYPERION BOOKS
NEW YORK

Special thanks to Frederick J. Booth, Ph.D.,
Professor of Classical Studies, Seton Hall University,
for his expert advice

This edition, 2010
3 5 7 9 10 8 6 4
V567-9638-5- 12013
Printed in the United States of America
ISBN 978-1-4231-2610-2
Visit www.hyperionbooksforchildren.com

THIS LABEL APPLIES TO TEXT STOCK

For Chip Hughes

CONTENTS

BOOK FOUR

BOOK FIVE

BOOK SIX

Book Four

THE GRAY-EYED
GODDESS

PROLOGUE

*I*n the early morning of time, there existed a mysterious world called Mount Olympus. Hidden behind a veil of clouds, this world was never swept by winds, nor washed by rains. Those who lived on Mount Olympus never grew old; they never died. They were not humans. They were the mighty gods and goddesses of ancient Greece.

The Olympian gods and goddesses had great power over the lives of the humans who lived on earth below. Their anger once caused a man named Odysseus to wander the seas for many long years, trying to find his way home.

Almost three thousand years ago, a Greek poet named Homer first told the story of Odysseus' journey. Since that time, storytellers have told the strange and wondrous tale again and again. We call that story the Odyssey.

ODYSSEUS AND PENELOPE

*O*dysseus, king of Ithaca, walked slowly along the shore of the wooded island. As he stared at the restless sea, he yearned for his distant homeland. He had not seen his island of Ithaca,

or his family, for almost twenty years—
not since he had sailed away to fight in
the Trojan War. He mourned his ill luck
since the war's end.

Perhaps I would be home in Ithaca now,
he thought, *if the Greeks had not angered
Athena, the warrior goddess, and caused
our ships to be blown off course . . . or if I
had not angered Poseidon, the god of the
seas, by blinding his son, the Cyclops . . . or
if my men had not angered the god of the
winds or the god of the sun. . . .*

Odysseus sighed with sorrow and
despair. All his men were dead now,

struck down by the wrath of the gods for their grievous sins. He alone had been spared. His strength and courage had helped him survive the horrors of war and the perils of his journey toward home.

Now Odysseus felt as if he were living in a nightmare from which he could not wake. For seven long years, the sea goddess Calypso had kept him captive on her island. Every day she tried to make him forget his past with her honey-sweet words. She promised him anything, if only he would marry her. She paid no heed to his protests that he still loved his true wife, Penelope, and their son, Telemachus.

And what is happening to my family now? Odysseus wondered.

He remembered the words the ghost of his mother had spoken when he journeyed to the Land of the Dead: *"Your family has been broken by sorrow. Your wife still waits for you. But she spends her days and nights weeping. Your son is strong and brave. Though he is young, he guards your home, your fields, and your livestock. He also mourns your absence, as does your father...."*

It had been many years since his mother's spirit had spoken those words. Did his father still live? And what had become of his son? Telemachus had been a baby when Odysseus left Ithaca. Now he would be a young man of twenty.

And was Penelope still faithful? Or had she cast off all memory of Odysseus and married another?

Desperate to go back to Ithaca and be reunited with his family, Odysseus stared at the wine-dark waves and prayed for a ship to take him home.

Far, far away from Calypso's island, Odysseus' wife, Penelope, stood at her tower window listening to the rowdy suitors in the courtyard below.

Penelope shuddered. For the last four years, suitors had traveled from near and far, seeking her hand in marriage. She despised them all. She knew it was not her they truly wanted—it was Odysseus' farms and fields, his livestock and servants, his rule over the island.

When the suitors had first come, Penelope had thought of a clever plan to ward them off. She told them she could not remarry until she finished weaving a shroud for the Odysseus' father to wear when he died. Every day she sat at her loom, weaving the garment. But every night, by torchlight, she unraveled all her day's work.

For three years, Penelope carried out her deception, yearning for her husband to return. But in the fourth year, one of her maids told the suitors of her trick.

The suitors were furious. They demanded that Penelope pick one of them to be her new husband. Still, Penelope refused. None of the greedy, rude men could ever compare to her lost Odysseus.

Even after so many years, she could still clearly picture her beloved: his proud posture, his broad shoulders, his auburn hair and lively, darting eyes. She felt the spirit of Odysseus whenever she looked about their house—in the wood-work he had trimmed with silver and gold and ivory; in the special bed he had carved for them. Odysseus had built their bedroom around an olive tree. He had cut the limbs off the tree and used its trunk for one of the bedposts.

Only he and Penelope knew this secret.

Penelope desperately wished for Odysseus to return and take swift, fierce action against the villains who were trying to take his place. Without her husband, there was no one to protect her.

Odysseus' father was too aged and feeble to help. Lost in grief, the old man wandered the island, never coming near the palace.

Telemachus, Penelope's son, was too young to help her. He had his father's bright eyes and auburn hair, but not his strength or cunning. Lately, the suitors had grown more and more scornful of Telemachus. They had also grown angrier and more insistent that Penelope choose one of them for a husband.

As rude laughter came from the courtyard, Penelope closed the shutters of her window. She returned to her loom and began weaving.

Desperate for help, she prayed for her true husband to come home soon, before it was too late.

SON OF ODYSSEUS

$\mathcal{T}$elemachus despised his mother's suitors even more than Penelope herself did. Every day, they invaded his father's estate. They slaughtered Odysseus' oxen, his long-horned cattle, his sheep, and his pigs. They stole wine from his vineyards and gave orders to his servants. Whenever Telemachus told them to leave, they laughed and mocked him.

Now, in the afternoon light, the suitors were sprawled about the courtyard, resting on the hides of oxen they had killed. They were playing dice and drinking from huge bowls of wine.

If my father would only come home, Telemachus thought, *he would quickly drive them all away and restore his rule over the island.*

Lost in his angry thoughts, Telemachus

did not notice for a moment that a stranger was waiting patiently at the threshold of the house. The stranger wore glittering gold sandals and carried a bronze spear.

When Telemachus finally saw the stranger, he jumped from his chair and hurried to welcome him. "Good day, sir!" he cried. "I am sorry you have been kept waiting at our gate!"

The stranger did not speak. He stared at Telemachus with piercing gray eyes.

"Come in, come in!" said Telemachus, ushering the stranger into the courtyard. "Refresh yourself with food and drink.

Then you must tell me from where you have come and what you seek."

Telemachus led the stranger quickly past the suitors in the courtyard and into the great hall. He wanted to protect his guest from the suitors' rudeness and noise.

"Please sit here," Telemachus said. He gestured to a tall, carved chair draped with the finest cloth. "Rest your feet on this stool."

Telemachus sat next to his guest. Servants brought trays of meat and bread. They poured wine and fresh water into golden goblets.

Soon Penelope's suitors began barging into the hall. They had come to hear music, sing songs, and dance. Telemachus was eager to ask questions of the visiting stranger, but he waited for the music to begin so the suitors would not hear his conversation.

As soon as the music and singing started, Telemachus leaned close to his gray-eyed guest.

"Tell me, sir, who are you?" the young man asked. "Where have you come from? What sort of ship brought you here? Are you a stranger to this house? Did you ever know my father, Odysseus, king of this island?"

"My name is Mentor," said the stranger. "I am chief of Taphos. Your father was a friend of mine, but I have not seen him since he left to fight the Trojan War. Recently I heard that he had come home, so I traveled here to Ithaca to see him again. I wanted to celebrate his safe return."

Telemachus lowered his head. "I am sorry to say my father has not returned," he said, "and we have had no word of him. I fear he has met with an ill fate and we shall never see him again."

"Perhaps the gods are only keeping him away for a while," said Mentor. "Perhaps he is a prisoner on an island somewhere. I am not a soothsayer, but deep within my heart, the gods whisper to me that your father is not dead. Remember, he is a man of great courage and strength. Even if he were in chains, he would eventually break free of them and find his way home."

Telemachus sighed. He dared not believe Mentor's words could be true. So many times over the years, his hopes about his father had been dashed.

The noise grew louder in the hall. All the suitors were singing now, and shouting, and making rude remarks.

Mentor looked at them. "Who are these men who swagger about your home?" he asked Telemachus. "Why do they behave in such a coarse and disgusting manner?"

"Sir, when my father was here, his estate was a safe and civilized place," said Telemachus. "But after he had been gone for some years, men from nearby islands began to invade our home. Now they slaughter and eat my father's livestock. They harass my mother and demand that she choose one of them to marry."

Mentor's eyes flashed with anger. "Odysseus must come home soon," he said in a low voice. "I have witnessed your father's strength. If he were here now, he would quickly punish these villains."

"Yes, I know he would," said Telemachus. "That is why I ache for his return. They will not listen to anything I say. I even fear they may soon try to kill me."

"My boy, you must gather your strength and courage," said Mentor, his voice shaking with anger. "You must find a way to deal with these men. Call them together tomorrow and order them to leave at once. Then gather a crew of twenty good men. Take the best ship you can find and set sail immediately in search of your father."

Telemachus was amazed by the vehemence of his guest. "I—I do not know how to search for him," he said.

"Sail to Pylos first," said Mentor. "Go to the home of wise Nestor. He was your father's friend and a brave warrior in the Trojan War. Ask Nestor about Odysseus. He will tell you what he knows, or he will tell you who else to ask."

"And what then?" asked Telemachus.

"If you learn that Odysseus has died, return home and mourn for him. Help your mother make plans to marry again. Kill those suitors who will not leave your estate."

Telemachus was frightened by the thought of such a challenge.

As if he could read Telemachus'

thoughts, Mentor leaned closer and looked deep into the young man's eyes. "Make a name for yourself, Telemachus," he said, "so people will praise your brave spirit. You are a man now, not a boy."

Telemachus felt heartened by the advice from Mentor. "Sir, you have been most kind to talk to me in this way," he said. "I feel almost as if you are my own father talking to me. I will do exactly as you say."

Mentor stood up to leave. "Now I must go back to my ship and crew," he said.

"Oh, please stay longer," implored Telemachus. "Rest, refresh yourself. Let me give you gifts to take with you."

"Nay, do not keep me," said Mentor. "I will receive your gifts when I stop here again. But now I must be on my way."

With these words, the gray-eyed stranger vanished as swiftly as a bird taking flight on the wind.

Telemachus was filled with wonder. He realized he'd been in the presence of a divine being.

THREE

THE GRAY-EYED GODDESS

*I*nspired by Mentor's words, Telemachus
was determined to throw the suitors out of
his house, once and for all.

They had quieted down a bit. A musician was playing his lyre and singing

about the Greeks returning from the Trojan War. He sang about Athena's anger and how she had told the gods to punish the Greek warriors. He sang about the storms that had blown their ships off course.

As the man sang his sad song, Telemachus saw his mother come down the steep stairway from her chambers. Two loyal handmaidens walked behind her.

Penelope stood in the shadows, listening. Though her face was covered by a veil, Telemachus could see that she wept.

Before the song was over, she lifted

her veil. "Singer, sing a different song!" she cried out. "I cannot endure your tale. It breaks my heart."

Telemachus stepped over to his mother. Inspired by his talk with Mentor, he spoke in a strong, calm voice.

"Let him sing on, Mother," he said. "He is not the cause of our sorrow. Only Zeus can bring such grief to mankind. Go back upstairs to your loom. Do not worry about our estate. From now on, I will be the master of my father's house."

Penelope was astonished by Telemachus' bold and decisive words. "In this moment, you truly seem the son of Odysseus," she said.

Penelope began to weep again. Such a vivid reminder of her husband made her even more sorrowful than before.

As her handmaidens helped Penelope back up the stairs, the suitors shouted after her, begging her to choose one of them to marry.

Telemachus turned to them. "You are shameless!" he said. "Enjoy the music and dancing tonight. But tomorrow morning I shall command you to leave our house. From then on, you will steal from another table—not mine, and not my mother's."

Amazed by Telemachus' bold speech, the suitors did not speak at first. But when they recovered, they were quick to show they were not afraid. Antinous, leader of the suitors, smiled mockingly. "Such bold words, Telemachus," he said. "I pray the gods never make *you* ruler over this island."

Telemachus stood his ground. "Antinous, with the gods' blessings, I *will* have command over all that my father has fought for and won," he said.

"Let the heavens decide who will be

the rightful king of Ithaca, then," said another suitor. "But tell us about the stranger who was just here. From what country had he come? What family? Did he bring news of your father? He hurried away so quickly, we could not get to know him."

"He was Mentor, an old friend of my father," answered Telemachus. "He came to inquire about my father's return— which he believes will be very soon."

The suitors laughed and shook their heads. Then they turned back to the sweetly lulling music. Lost in their idle pleasure, they took no more heed of the son of Odysseus.

Telemachus left the great hall and headed toward his bedroom. His old nursemaid, Euryclea, carried two blazing torches to light his way.

Euryclea loved Telemachus as her own child, for she had cared for him since he was an infant. In his room, she prepared his bed and carefully put away his clothes. Then she left him alone with his thoughts.

Telemachus lay under a soft woolen fleece and stared into the dark. His mind burned with a question: *Is it possible that Mentor is the goddess Athena in disguise?*

Telemachus remembered the story told to him since he was a child: Before the Greeks had angered Athena, she had favored Odysseus above all other men. She had told him how to build the Trojan horse so the Greeks could lay siege to the city of Troy.

Had Athena finally taken pity on the man she had once loved? Had she disguised herself as Mentor and come to save Odysseus' wife and son?

After all, Mentor's bronze-tipped

spear was very like the spear of the goddess. His glittering gold sandals were
like the magic sandals that carried her
through the air.

And did not his gray eyes shine like
the bright eyes of the goddess herself?

For the first time in months, Telemachus
allowed hope to enter his heart. He felt
certain the gray-eyed goddess had been
with him today. She had come to help
him find his father.

SETTING SAIL

*T*he next morning, Telemachus rose with the first light. In the rosy dawn, he dressed himself in his royal robe. He put on his sandals and strapped on his sword.

When he looked in his dressing

mirror, he was startled by his own appearance. He looked as handsome and powerful as a young god. Had Athena transformed him, he wondered, so he would shine before the others?

He bade his servants assemble all the men of Ithaca, including all the suitors. Then, with a spear in his hand and two hounds at his side, he went to meet the crowd.

As Telemachus moved through the throng of men, they all seemed to notice his changed appearance. Even the oldest among them made way for him.

Telemachus took his place at his father's seat and looked about at all those who had come to hear his words. As he rose to speak, he could hardly contain his emotions.

"You are demanding that my mother marry against her will," he said. "Day after day, you gather at this estate. You slaughter my father's livestock and drink his wine. He is not here to defend his home. I shall never be as strong a man as he was. Yet I cannot bear such treatment from you any longer. My father's house is falling into ruin—"

As Telemachus spoke, his newfound confidence began to fail him. "I—I ask you to respect your consciences and fear the wrath of heaven," he said in a trembling voice. Then, overpowered by his feelings, he dashed his spear to the ground and burst into tears.

From the looks on their faces, it seemed that some of the suitors had begun to feel true pity for Telemachus. The leader of the suitors, Antinous, stood up. "Blame your mother, Telemachus, not us," he said softly. "She deceived us. She said she could not choose a husband until she had woven a shroud for your grand-father. But every night she unraveled her day's work so the shroud would never be finished. For three years, she lied to us in this way. You must force her now to choose one of us to marry. We will not leave until she does."

Telemachus shook his head. "I cannot do as you say, Antinous," he said. "If you keep preying upon this house, I will ask Zeus for his help, and—and all of you will die."

As Telemachus spoke, a pair of eagles appeared overhead. Gliding on the currents of the wind, they circled the courtyard. Then they began furiously beating the air with their wings. They gave a death stare to those below. Then, suddenly, they turned on each other. They fought fiercely for a moment, then flew off into the sky.

The men murmured with alarm: "What can this mean? What is Zeus telling us?"

A wise old man stood up. He spoke in a shaky voice. "Men of Ithaca, I see an omen in the eagles," he said. "Zeus is telling us that Odysseus will not stay away much longer. Unless those who pursue his wife leave of their own accord, all our deaths are at hand. Let them be gone from this place before it is too late!"

But the suitors refused to heed the warning.

"Go home, old man!" one shouted. "Birds are always flying about! It means nothing! We shall stay here as long as we like! Odysseus is dead! We do not fear his son with his fine speeches!"

Telemachus shook his head. "The gods know my story," he said. "So here is what I propose to you. Give me a ship and a crew of twenty, and I shall set out in search of my father. If I hear that he is alive, we shall all wait patiently for his return. If I hear he is dead, we will have a funeral for him, and my mother will choose which one of you she will marry."

But the suitors would not agree even to this simple plan. Instead, they mocked Telemachus, saying he was not strong enough to survive such a voyage.

Then they returned to the halls of the palace to feast and drink while they waited for Penelope to make her choice.

In despair, Telemachus walked alone

down to the sea. He washed his hands in the foamy water and prayed to the goddess Athena for help.

"I know you came to me yesterday and bade me take a ship to search for my father," he said. "Tell me now what I should do! My mother's suitors scorn me! And now I fear no one in all of Ithaca will aid me in my quest."

In a flash, Mentor was at his side. His gray eyes glinting, he spoke plainly: "Telemachus, you have shown this morning that you indeed have a bit of your father's strength and courage. So I will help you on your journey. Think no more of the wicked ones who stand in your way. Believe me, on their day, they will pay for their rude disrespect. Return home, pack wine and provisions for your voyage to Nestor's island of Pylos. I will find men to sail with you. I will find the best ship and launch it upon the sea."

Telemachus thanked Mentor, and with great haste, he returned alone to his father's estate. When he arrived there, he found the suitors slaughtering goats and pigs in the courtyard.

They jeered at Telemachus as he passed by. "Boaster!" "Pretender!"

Telemachus ignored them and went straight to the storeroom where Odysseus kept his gold and bronze, and his finest clothes and oils and wines. Day and night, the storeroom was watched over by Telemachus' old nursemaid, Euryclea.

Telemachus now sought help from Euryclea. He asked her to pour wine into kegs and barley meal into bags.

"Keep these provisions hidden till nightfall," he told the old woman. "When it grows dark, I will collect them and take them to a ship that waits for me. I am sailing to Pylos tonight in search of news of my father. Promise not to tell my mother for at least ten days. If she knows my plan, she will try to stop me."

Euryclea cried out in distress. "Please do not go, my boy! These wicked men will be angry when they learn that you have left! They will find you and murder you!"

"No, I will be safe," Telemachus assured the old woman, "for this is the will of the goddess Athena. She is helping me."

Indeed, even as Telemachus spoke to Euryclea, the gray-eyed goddess was moving quickly about the city. Disguised as Telemachus himself, she found twenty good men to row his ship to Pylos.

When evening came and the streets were dark, Athena put a ship upon the sea and equipped it with all it needed for sailing. Then, disguised again as Mentor, she met the crew as they arrived at the dock.

Mentor set each man to work on the ship, then hurried to the house of Odysseus and put a spell of sleep upon all who were there, except Telemachus.

Still in the guise of Mentor, Athena

called to him from the great hall. "Your men and your ship are at the port. Let us go."

Telemachus hurried after Mentor. When he came to the shore, he found the crew of twenty waiting for him. With dignity and calm, the son of Odysseus gave them their orders: "Make haste to my house. Wake not a soul. No one else knows of our plan. Bring our provisions down to the shore."

Telemachus' crew quickly did as he ordered. Soon they were ready to cast off their anchor and set sail. Telemachus and Mentor took their seats in the stern of the vessel.

From the bright gray eyes of the goddess came a western wind. It rippled over the sea.

"Catch the ropes! Hoist the sail!" Telemachus called.

The crew lifted the mast and hauled up a white sail.

The wind blew full blast, and a dark wave sent the ship on its way. The men poured wine to honor the gods, most especially Athena, mighty daughter of Zeus.

Little do they know, thought Telemachus, *that the goddess herself sails with us tonight.*

FIVE

THE SEARCH

*F*rom dark till dawn, Telemachus' ship sped on its way toward King Nestor's island of Pylos.

Just as the sun was rising above the sea, the ship reached its port. A great crowd was gathered on the beach. They were offering sacrifices to Poseidon, lord of the seas.

The crew lowered their sail. Mentor ordered them to stay aboard, while he and Telemachus went ashore in search of King Nestor.

As they walked together, Mentor offered advice to the young man: "Do not be shy before the king," he said. "Ask him for news of your father—is he dead? And if so, where is he buried? Beg him to tell you the truth, for he is wise and powerful beyond all men."

Telemachus drew back, afraid to approach such a great man. King Nestor had been a fearless warrior and sailor, a master horseman, and a killer of giants. Most of all, he was known for his great wisdom and judgment.

"Do not worry," said Mentor. "Heaven will prompt you. Believe me when I tell you that the gods have been with you since the moment of your birth."

Hearing these words, Telemachus gathered his courage. When he and Mentor reached the crowd on the shore, they saw Nestor sitting with his seven sons as others prepared a great feast.

Two of Nestor's sons rushed forward to welcome the two strangers to their island. They invited them to sit on soft sheepskins. They served them meat on silver platters and wine in golden cups.

When Mentor and Telemachus had finished eating and drinking, Nestor approached them. "It is proper to ask questions of guests only after they have had their fill of food and wine," he said. "So now that you have feasted with us, tell me: Who are you? From what land have you sailed? Are you traders or pirates?"

Mentor nodded to Telemachus, encouraging him to speak boldly.

"We come from Ithaca, the island once ruled by the brave Odysseus," Telemachus said. "We come in search of news of him. We want to learn of his fate when he sailed for home after the Trojan War. Please, tell us what you know. Do not soften the story. I must know the truth, for I am his son."

Nestor gasped with astonishment. "I can hardly believe my eyes," the old man said. "But now that you tell me who you are, I see that you indeed look very like your father, Odysseus. I will tell you all I know of his journeys and adventures.

"When we set sail from Troy, Athena was angry with some of the Greeks for defiling her temple in the heat of battle. At her bidding, Zeus scattered our fleet and flung our ships far away from each other on the open seas. I finally found my way back home, but knew nothing of the fate of my comrades. I could not say who had been saved or who had been lost. All I know of their fates is what I have since learned in the halls of my own palace. I am sorry, but no news of your father has ever come to me."

Telemachus sighed with despair. Then he told his father's old friend about the suitors who had invaded his home and were stealing his father's provisions.

Nestor was silent for a moment. He seemed deep in thought. Finally he spoke in a soft, steady voice.

"I will tell you what you should do now," he said. "Go to the palace of King Menelaus and beautiful Queen Helen. Menelaus was the last to arrive home from the Trojan War. He has traveled to many lands. Beg him to tell you all he knows. He will not deceive you."

Telemachus thanked Nestor for his counsel. Then Nestor invited Telemachus and Mentor to rest at his house for the night. "The son of mighty Odysseus and his friend need not sleep on the deck of a ship tonight!" he said.

Mentor stood up. "Thank you, but I fear I must return to our ship and take care of our crew. Telemachus will stay and sleep in your home. Please, lend him your swiftest horses and finest chariot, so that he might travel to the palace of Menelaus tomorrow."

Then, with these words, Athena suddenly took her leave—not as Mentor, but in the winged shape of a mighty eagle.

All who saw the sight were struck dumb with amazement. Nestor gasped and grabbed Telemachus' hand. "My friend," he said, "you travel with the gods themselves! I believe your friend was in truth the gray-eyed daughter of Zeus!"

Nestor prayed to Athena and promised to sacrifice a prized heifer in her honor. Then the old man led Telemachus to a lofty room of his palace where his servants had prepared a comfortable bed.

Telemachus rose early the next morning. He was bathed and anointed with oil. Then, dressed in a fine tunic and cloak, he left the palace of King Nestor to begin his journey.

Again, all who saw Telemachus were amazed, for he looked like a young god.

Nestor ordered that his swiftest horses be yoked to his finest chariot. He ordered his servants to pack provisions of meat, bread, and wine.

Then he bade his youngest son to travel with Telemachus to the palace of King Menelaus.

The two young men climbed into the chariot. Nestor's son took hold of the reins and snapped them sharply, and the team of horses galloped away.

All day the horses sped like the wind over the plains. When the sun went down and darkness spread over the land, they rested.

The next morning as dawn showed her rosy fingers in the sky, the two young men yoked the horses again and flew through fields of wheat and corn.

Again, the swift horses galloped all day. At nightfall, they came to a palace deep in a valley, the home of King Menelaus and beautiful Queen Helen.

THE OLD MAN OF THE SEA

*T*he horses stopped at the gate of
the palace. Telemachus and Nestor's son
could hear sounds of a celebration coming from inside.

Servants greeted the two strangers at

the gate. The young men were welcomed and treated as grandly as royal visitors. Telemachus knew that this was the custom of all the Greeks. Wandering travelers received the greatest courtesy, for a man never knew when he himself might be a stranger in another's house.

Servants washed and anointed the two young men with sweet-smelling oil. They gave them the finest purple robes. Then they led them into the great hall.

Telemachus marveled at what he saw there. The splendor seemed greater than that of the sun or the moon.

Telemachus and Nestor's son were seated near the king. They were served rich foods and golden goblets filled with wine.

"Welcome," said King Menelaus. "Have your supper; then you shall tell me who you are and from where you have come."

As Telemachus ate, he looked about the great hall. The room gleamed with bronze, gold, and amber, and with ivory and silver.

"This palace seems like the very home of Zeus," he whispered to his friend.

King Menelaus overheard Telemachus' words. "Ah, I must not be compared with a god of Olympus," he said. "After the Trojan War, I traveled to many countries and gathered many treasures. But none of them take away the sorrow I still feel for my comrades who were slain by the Trojans, or who died on their voyages home.

"There is one I grieve for more than all the rest, for I have heard how his family still aches for his return. His mother died of her grief. His wife and his father have nearly gone mad with sorrow. Even his son mourns night and day for him, though the boy was but a babe when his father sailed away to war."

Telemachus covered his face to hide his tears. The king had perfectly described the family of Odysseus.

At that moment, Queen Helen came down from her perfumed room and entered the hall. Looking as beautiful as the most exquisite goddess, she took her seat beside the king.

"Who are these strangers?' she asked her husband. "Does not one of them look remarkably like the great Odysseus?"

Nestor's son nodded. "Indeed, this is the son of Odysseus," he said. "He is shy in your presence. My father, Nestor, has sent me with him to seek news of his father. In all Ithaca there is no one to help him fight the injustices he faces."

Menelaus was greatly moved to learn the identity of his young guest.

"Your father was much loved," he told Telemachus.

Then the king and queen, Telemachus, and even the son of Nestor wept for the lost warrior.

"He was a great warrior," said Helen.

"When I was held captive in Troy, it was his bravery and cunning that rescued me."

"Aye," said Menalaus. "I remember well how he dared to hide in the great wooden horse. Under the cover of night, he unlocked the gates of Troy, so we could lay siege to the city."

Telemachus nodded. "Your majesty, my father was very brave indeed," he said sadly, "but all his courage and cunning could not save him from his fate. Let us go to our beds now and seek peace from this sorrow in sleep."

Queen Helen ordered her maids to

make beds for the guests in the gallery of the palace. Servants led the two young men from the great hall by torch-light and offered them blankets and fine woolen gowns. Weary from their long journey, Telemachus and the son of Nestor finally lay down to rest.

Before dawn, Menelaus rose and went to the place where Telemachus slept. He woke the young man and spoke softly to him. "Tell me exactly why you came to see me in my palace," he said. "How can I help you?"

Telemachus told the king about the

suitors who had greedily moved into his father's home.

"If your father knew this," said Menelaus, "he would tear them to pieces."

"Do you have news of him?" asked Telemachus. "Can you tell me anything? Pray, do not soften your words."

"I will tell you what I know," said the king. "There is an island in the sea near Egypt where many voyagers stop to rest before sailing on. My ship landed there after the war. I was lost and did not know if any of my comrades had jour-neyed safely back home. One day, while

I was wandering alone, a sea nymph told me to speak to her father, the Old Man of the Sea."

"Who is he?" asked Telemachus.

"He is a sea god," said Menelaus. "He is Poseidon's herdsman, who tends to the seals. There is a time of day when he rises to the surface to count his flocks. To catch him, one must hold him fast, for he can change his shape into many forms. He can be any of the creatures that move about the earth. He can be water or fire. But if you can hold him fast, when he is himself again, you may ask him your questions."

"And did you catch this strange sea god?" Telemachus asked with wonder.

"Yes, I waited until he emerged to count his seals. Then I rushed upon him and seized him," said the king. "He quickly turned into a lion, then a snake, then a leopard, then a boar. He became running water, and then a tree. But I held him fast until he changed back into himself again. When I asked him how I might get home, he gave me wise advice.

"When I asked about the fate of my friends, he told me about those who had died. When I wept with grief, he told me that one great warrior was still alive. He said that Odysseus was trapped on the island of Calypso. The goddess was keeping him there against his will."

Telemachus rejoiced to hear that his father must still be alive.

Menelaus told him more about his journeys, then took his leave. Left alone, Telemachus was restless with excitement.

Is my father still on Calypso's island? he wondered. *Should I go in search of him there? Or should I return home at once and tell my mother the good news?*

SEVEN

CALYPSO'S ISLAND

*F*ar away on Calypso's island, Odysseus sat on a rock and wept. On this day, like all others for the past seven years, he yearned for home.

With his face buried in his hands, he

did not see the bright light swoop through the air and skim the waves like a gull. He did not see Hermes, the messenger god, take shape before him.

Carrying his golden spear, and wearing his golden winged sandals, Hermes began moving lightly over the island. He stepped through Calypso's sacred woods, where owls, falcons, and seagulls called from the branches of alders, poplars, and cypresses.

He moved through Calypso's sweet-smelling garden, over beds of violets and herbs. Finally he came to the entrance of the goddess's cave.

Hermes pushed past the hanging grape vines and stepped inside. The scent of cedar and sandalwood filled the air.

The fair-haired goddess was sitting at her loom before her hearth, singing a song. When she looked up, she gave the messenger god a radiant smile.

"Hermes, you have honored me with a visit!" she said. "Sit and let me offer you food and drink."

Calypso served Hermes ambrosia and red nectar, food for the gods. After he had refreshed himself, Hermes told Calypso the purpose of his visit.

"Today on Olympus, the goddess Athena called together all the gods," he said. "She is greatly worried about Odysseus, king of Ithaca. He has been kept from his home and family too long, she says, and now his enemies are planning to murder his son. Calypso, Zeus has heard the words of his daughter. He commands you to release your captive."

The goddess rose in anger, but Hermes continued: "Zeus has decreed that Odysseus must return home on his own strength. No god is allowed to speed his journey. He must build a raft and ride the waves for twenty days to the land of Scheria. From there, he can sail on to Ithaca and avenge the wrongs done to his family."

"The gods of Olympus are angry with me," said Calypso. "They do not like to believe a goddess can fall in love with a mortal man! But I saved Odysseus' life!"

Calypso stared fiercely at Hermes for a moment. Then she lowered her eyes in defeat. "I know I cannot defy the will of Zeus," she said. "If Zeus commands it, Odysseus shall leave my island. In all good faith, I will give him the advice he needs to begin his journey home."

Hermes bowed. Then he took swift leave of the mournful goddess.

Calypso set out to look for Odysseus. She found him on the rocks, weeping. She sat beside him and spoke gently.

"You shall no longer stay here, yearning for your home," she said. "I will send you away. Go, cut beams of wood. Make a large raft to carry you over the sea. I will give you wine, bread, water, and clothing."

After his many years of being held captive, Odysseus did not trust

Calypso's words. "Not even a well-made ship could safely sail these waves," he said. "Will you swear a sacred oath that you are not trying to harm me?"

The goddess took his hand. "I swear by heaven and earth and by the waters of the Underworld that I want no harm to come to you, Odysseus," she said.

Having sworn her oath, Calypso rose and quickly walked away. Odysseus followed her to her cave. Calypso bade her servants prepare a meal. Her hand-maidens served her ambrosia and nectar, food for the deathless gods. Calypso herself served Odysseus meat and wine, refreshment for mere mortals.

"Odysseus, if you would only promise to stay with me and marry me, I would make you, too, an immortal being," Calypso said. "You would live forever."

"Fair goddess, why would I want to live forever far from my home, without my wife and son?" he asked.

"I cannot imagine that your wife is more beautiful than I am," said Calypso.

"Goddess, do not be angry with me," said Odysseus. "What you say is true.

My wife is a mortal woman. She is not as beautiful as you. Still, for seven years, I have thought of nothing but getting home to her."

Desperate to keep Odysseus on her island, Calypso gave him one more reason to stay. "If you sail for home, Odysseus, you will find many troubles along the way, for the gods will not aid your journey," she said. "They will test your powers of endurance, again and again."

"Should the gods choose to destroy my raft, I shall bear it," said Odysseus.

"I have suffered many hardships and can certainly endure one more."

Calypso sighed and nodded. She could see that she had no choice. She had to let Odysseus go.

The next morning, at dawn, Calypso dressed in a beautiful shimmering silver gown. She covered her head with a veil. Then she gave Odysseus a sharp ax made of bronze and led him to the far end of the island.

There, many tall trees grew—aspens and pines that reached as high as the sky.

"Cut what you need for your ship," the goddess said.

For the next four days, Odysseus cut down trees with his bronze ax. He worked until he had felled twenty. Then he set about building his raft.

He smoothed the felled timbers and fixed them together with wooden bolts. Then he built a deck and made a mast and a steering rudder. Calypso gave him linen cloth for a sail. When the sea craft was finally finished, Odysseus used logs to roll it down to the water.

On the fifth day after Hermes' visit

to Calypso, Odysseus was ready to set sail. Calypso gave him clean clothes. She gave him goatskins filled with deep-red wine and water and meat. She told him which stars he should follow to guide his way.

The goddess hid her grief as Odysseus moved away from her into the water and climbed aboard his raft.

The last gift Calypso gave Odysseus was a fair, warm wind to send his raft safely out to sea.

THE VOYAGE

With his hands gripping the rudder, Odysseus skillfully guided his raft over the waves. He never slept. All night, he kept his eyes fixed on the stars that Calypso had told him to watch—the Pleiades and the Bear.

Day after day and night after night, Odysseus sailed the seas. Finally, on the eighteenth day, he saw the dim outline of mountains on the horizon.

As Odysseus steered his raft toward the shore, dark clouds gathered overhead. The water began to rise. The wind began to blow, until it was roaring over the earth and sea.

Has Poseidon discovered my raft? Odysseus wondered anxiously. *Does he now seek his final revenge?*

For many years, Poseidon, mighty

ruler of the sea, had been angry with Odysseus for blinding his son, the Cyclops. Now it seemed he was trying to destroy Odysseus once again. The wind roared from the north, south, east, and west. Daylight plunged into darkness. Odysseus feared he was about to come to a terrible, lonely end.

Suddenly an enormous wave crashed down on Odysseus' raft. Odysseus was swept overboard and pulled deep beneath the sea. He struggled wildly to raise his head above the water and breathe.

When his head finally broke the

surface, Odysseus saw his raft swiftly moving away across the water. He swam as fast as he could toward the wooden craft. He grabbed the timbers and pulled himself aboard.

Then, as the wind swirled the raft across the water, Odysseus saw an astonishing sight. A sea goddess was floating like a gull on top of the waves.

Seemingly impervious to the great storm, she floated near his raft and climbed aboard.

"My friend," she said, "I am Ino, the White Goddess, who guides sailors in storms. I know not why Poseidon is angry with you. But I know this: for all the torture he has inflicted upon you, he will not kill you. But you must leave your raft at once and swim for the shore. Take my veil, for it is enchanted. You will come to no harm as long as you possess it. As soon as you reach land, you must throw it back into the sea."

With these words, the White Goddess removed her enchanted veil and gave it to Odysseus. Then she disappeared back into the wild seas.

At that moment, a huge wave crashed

down on Odysseus' raft, ripping it to pieces. Clutching Ino's veil, Odysseus pulled himself onto a wooden plank and rode it as if it were a horse. Then he dove down into the sea.

Suddenly, all the winds died down—except the north wind. Odysseus felt that Athena was holding the other winds back, so he could swim safely and swiftly to some distant shore. For two days and two nights, with the north wind gently flattening the waves before him, he swam and floated on the calm sea.

On the third day, the north wind

died away and the sea was completely calm. Odysseus saw land ahead. With a burst of joy, he swam toward the rocky shore.

In an instant, the wind and waves returned. With a thundering roar, sea spray rained down on him.

Odysseus struggled to keep his head above the churning water, seeking a place to go ashore.

Angry waves were pounding the reefs with great force. *I'll be dashed against the rocks if I try to swim ashore now*, he thought desperately.

But once again, Odysseus felt the presence of Athena. A giant wave picked him up and carried him over the rocks toward the beach. But before Odysseus could crawl ashore to safety, another wave dragged him back into the sea and pulled him under the water.

Odysseus swam desperately, escaping the waves pounding the shore. Soon he came to a sheltered cove. He saw a river-bank free of rough stones. As he swam toward the bank, he prayed to the gods to save him from the angry attack of Poseidon.

Suddenly the waves were still. But when Odysseus tried to haul himself ashore, his body failed him. He had been defeated by the storm. It had ripped his flesh and robbed his muscles of their strength. He was passing in and out of consciousness.

Gasping for breath, he pulled off Ino's veil and threw it back into the sea. Then he used his last bit of strength to drag himself out of the water and throw himself into the river reeds.

If I lie here all night, I shall die from the cold and damp, he thought. *If I go farther ashore and pass out in a thicket, wild beasts will devour me.* No matter what evils lay ahead, he knew he had to push on. On bleeding hands and knees, he crawled to a sheltered spot under an olive tree, a tree sacred to the goddess Athena.

Odysseus lay down in a pile of dead leaves. With his bloody hands, he spread leaves over his torn body. Like a farmer spreading ashes over the embers of his fire, he tried to protect the last spark of life within him.

Mercifully, the gray-eyed goddess slipped down from the heavens and appeared at his side. She closed his weary eyes and pulled him down into a sweet sleep that took away his pain and sorrow.

EPILOGUE

Back in Ithaca, Penelope, the wife of Odysseus, opened her door and greeted a friend named Medon.

"I have just received terrible news," said Medon. "Your suitors, led by Antinous, are plotting against your son. They are waiting for him on the island of Asteris. When his ship sails past, they will kill him."

Penelope fell to the floor in a faint. When she came to, she wept bitterly. "Where is my boy?" she said between sobs. "I thought he was somewhere in the countryside."

"I know only that he set out some days ago in search of news of his father," said Medon. "Soon he will be sailing for home and crossing the path of his enemies."

Penelope was plunged into such despair that she could not rise from the floor. As she wept and wailed for her lost husband and her beloved son, all her handmaidens wept with her.

Euryclea, the aged nursemaid of Telemachus, tried to comfort her. "Call upon the goddess Athena!" she urged Penelope. "Ask for her help. She will save your boy!"

The old woman wiped away Penelope's tears. She helped her bathe and dressed her in clean linens. She helped her make an offering to the goddess.

Penelope prayed to Athena. "O daughter of Zeus, hear me," she said. "I beg you to keep my son safe from harm."

Exhausted and filled with grief,

Penelope then went to her chambers and lay down on her bed.

Mercifully, the gray-eyed goddess soon came. She closed Penelope's weary eyes and pulled her down into a sweet sleep that took away her pain and sorrow.

Book Five

RETURN TO ITHACA

SEPARATION AND SORROW

*B*eneath an olive tree on a strange shore lay Odysseus, the lost king of Ithaca. In the weeks before, Odysseus had fought for his life against a terrible storm. He had lived many days without food or fresh water. He had narrowly escaped death with the aid of a sea goddess. And now, covered by a blanket of leaves, he was drifting into a deep and exhausted sleep.

For the twenty years since he had left the battlefields of Troy, Odysseus had tried desperately to return to his beloved island of Ithaca. In that time, he had braved many storms and fought many monsters. He had lost his fleet of twelve ships and all of his men.

Odysseus ached always to return to his home and be reunited with his wife,

Penelope, and their son, Telemachus. Though he had not seen them in twenty years, they were ever in his heart and mind. But as he lay on this distant shore, it seemed impossible to Odysseus that he would ever get home. . . .

❧ ❧ ❧

As Odysseus slept on the beach, far away Penelope slept in her palace bed, weary from weeping. For many years, wicked men had invaded her husband's estate, demanding that she take one of them for a husband. Penelope had steadfastly refused, and now her suitors were plotting to kill her son as he returned home from searching for his father. Upon hearing this news, Penelope had collapsed. She could hardly bear her husband's absence. Surely she would die if she lost her son as well. . . .

Far away from Ithaca, Penelope's son, Telemachus, lay in a splendid chamber in the palace of the king and queen of Sparta. He had traveled there to find news of his father, and his quest had been fulfilled. King Menelaus had told him that Odysseus might be a captive on the island of the goddess Calypso.

Since receiving this news, Telemachus had been asking himself the same questions over and over: Should he set out in search of Calypso's island in hopes of finding his father? Or should he return to Ithaca and help his mother in her struggle against the suitors who were trying to take his father's place?

The son of Odysseus did not know that even now evil men were waiting to ambush him on his way home.

High on Mount Olympus, the gray-eyed goddess Athena looked down on Odysseus, Penelope, and Telemachus. Something must be done to save Odysseus and his wife and son, she thought—and quickly. So, in the hour before dawn, Athena left her bright, perfect world in the clouds and slipped down to the small and troubled world below. . . .

THE PRINCESS

Athena traveled swiftly over the earth to the land of King Alcinous. King Alcinous was a wise and generous leader, and his kingdom was blessed. The men were the best sailors in all the world, and the women were the best weavers.

Athena passed green fields, splendid temples, and lovely houses until finally she came to the palace of the king and queen. In the hour before dawn, she slipped through the entranceway, then down the hall to the chamber of the king's daughter, Nausicaa.

The goddess glided silently into the princess's room. Like a breath of wind, she swept past two young handmaidens sleeping near the door.

Athena hovered for a moment over the princess's bed. Then she quickly changed her shape to that of Nausicaa's closest friend. She spoke to the princess as if in a dream.

"Nausicaa, you are so lazy!" she said. "Don't you know that there are many dirty clothes in the palace that must be washed? How will you ever marry if you do not have a clean gown? At dawn, you must load the best linen into a wagon and go to the pools near the shore and do the washing!"

The gray-eyed goddess then slipped out of the palace as swiftly and silently as she had come.

When dawn broke, Nausicaa woke and remembered her strange dream. She hurried at once to her parents' chamber. "Father! I must go today and wash all our best clothes in the sea!" she said. "If I do not have clean clothes, how will I ever marry?"

King Alcinous smiled. He thought his daughter's words were strange, but he could refuse her nothing. "If that is what you wish, Nausicaa, that is what you shall do," he said. "I will tell the servants to fetch a wagon and harness the mules so you can carry all our clothes down to the sea."

The king's servants quickly prepared a wagon. The princess and her handmaidens loaded piles of soiled cloaks, robes, tunics, and gowns into the back. They packed a lunch of bread and meat, a goatskin filled with wine, and a flask of golden olive oil.

Nausicaa climbed into the driver's seat of the wagon and snapped the reins. The team of mules lunged forward and the wagon rattled noisily over the road, carrying the princess and her handmaidens toward the sea.

When they came to the washing pools

near the shore, the girls unhitched the mules. They unloaded the wagon and carried the piles of clothes down to the pools. They stamped on the garments, washing them in seawater until they were spotless. Then they spread them over the rocks to dry.

As they waited for the sun and wind to dry their laundry, the princess and her handmaidens bathed in the sea. They ate their bread and meat. Then they threw off their veils and began playing ball.

The princess tossed the ball high into the air. A maiden missed the catch, and the ball rolled into the water. As the girls ran to get it, they laughed and shouted.

Not far away, a sad and weary man lay beneath a blanket of leaves under an olive tree. When he heard the voices of the young girls, he opened his eyes.

Where am I? he wondered. *Who is shouting and laughing? Their voices sound like those of nymphs who haunt rivers and mountains.*

Odysseus broke off a bough of thick leaves to hide his nakedness. Then he crept out from under the olive tree into the afternoon sun.

THE STRANGER

*W*hen the handmaidens saw Odysseus, they screamed and ran away. But Princess Nausicaa stood very still, for Athena had filled her heart with courage. The young girl stared at the unkempt stranger, covered with sea salt and dirt and leaves.

"Beautiful princess, are you a goddess or a mortal?" Odysseus said. "Whoever you are, have pity on me, for I have suffered much. I was tossed upon the seas for twenty days, until the waves flung me onto this shore. Can you give me clothes to hide my nakedness? Can you tell me the way to your town?"

The princess drew close to Odysseus. "Stranger, I believe you are a good man," she said. "I am Nausicaa, the daughter of King Alcinous. My maids and I will help you."

Nausicaa called for her handmaidens to come out of their hiding places. She ordered them to bring clean clothes and olive oil for the mysterious stranger.

Odysseus washed himself in a stream, then rubbed the olive oil over his battered, sun-dried skin. When he had dressed himself in a tunic and cloak, the princess's handmaidens brought him meat and wine.

After Odysseus finished his meal, Princess Nausicaa told him what he must do. "You may follow our wagon to the walls of the town," she said, "but when we get inside the walls, you must leave us. The men of my land are the finest sailors in the world, but they are suspicious of strangers. They may think you are a vagabond from some foreign ship and speak ill of me for leading you to our city."

"Where should I go?" asked Odysseus.

"Inside the walls of the city there is a grove of poplars sacred to Athena. Wait there until I have had time to get home," said Nausicaa. "Then come to the palace. Inside you will find my parents sitting before a fire. My mother will be spinning dark-blue wool. Kneel before her and ask for help."

The princess then shook the reins of her wagon, and the mules began clattering toward town.

Odysseus followed the wagon past fields and farmland and a harbor filled with fine ships. When the wagon arrived at the narrow gates of the city, Odysseus followed it through the gates, then stopped and watched it rattle on without him.

Odysseus walked quickly through a marketplace filled with merchants selling fish, sails, and ship's oars. As he made his way between the stalls, several of the merchants and customers eyed him suspiciously. Odysseus quickly slipped past them and into the sacred grove of poplar trees. He hid among the trees, waiting for the princess to reach the palace.

While he waited, Odysseus prayed to the gods. "Hear me, O gods of Olympus! Have pity upon me," he begged. "Grant that I may make my way safely to the palace and find favor with the king and queen."

Odysseus remained hidden in the olive grove until he was sure Princess Nausicaa had had enough time to reach the palace.

Then he stepped cautiously out onto the city streets again.

As Odysseus started out of the grove, a strange mist covered his body. No one seemed to notice him as he made his way through the streets. *Has Athena made me invisible?* he wondered.

Suddenly a small girl stepped in front of Odysseus. The child stared up at him with bright gray eyes. Odysseus wondered if the girl might be Athena in disguise.

"Can you tell me the way to the palace of the king?" he asked her.

"I will show you," said the child. "Follow me and speak to no one."

Odysseus followed the girl through the streets. When they drew near the palace, she said simply, "Go inside and look for the queen." Then she disappeared, leaving Odysseus alone at the palace gates.

Odysseus entered the gates and passed through an orchard of trees laden with luscious figs, pears, and apples. He walked through a rich vineyard and a bountiful flower garden.

When he entered the halls of the palace, he gasped in wonder. The palace shone with a splendor like that of the sun and moon. Golden statues of boys holding fiery torches lit the halls. In the gleaming light, handmaidens worked at their looms. Their fingers fluttered like aspen leaves in the wind as they wove their beautiful linen.

No one seemed to notice Odysseus as he walked through the palace. Hidden by Athena's cloak of mist, he slipped silently into the great hall. As Odysseus looked about for the queen, he saw a group of nobles sitting near an open fire. Nearby sat the king and a woman spinning wool.

Odysseus moved quickly toward Nausicaa's mother. As he knelt in the ashes before the hearth, he felt the mist around him evaporate—and suddenly, he was visible again.

Some in the hall cried out in alarm when they saw the strange, haggard man. But Odysseus spoke quickly and passionately to the queen: "I humbly beg you to have pity on me!" he said. "I have come here from beyond the sea. Help me find my way back to my home country, to my wife and my son."

FOUR

THE FEAST

*E*veryone in the great hall stared in shock at Odysseus as he knelt before the queen. Finally an old man broke the silence. "We must honor our most ancient tradition," he said. "Almighty Zeus tells us never to deny a stranger who asks for our protection. Give this wretched man a chair. Offer him wine and supper."

King Alcinous helped Odysseus to a chair. A servant brought a silver basin and washed Odysseus' hands. Others brought him bread and meat and wine.

The king and queen and all their guests raised their cups in the air. "To Zeus, protector of worthy strangers," said the king. Then he looked at Odysseus. "Perhaps you are one of the immortals yourself, come down to earth to test our hospitality."

Odysseus shook his head. "Pray, sir, do not mistake me for a god. In truth, I am the most wretched of men. If only you knew what misery I have suffered."

King Alcinous seemed moved by Odysseus' humble words. He turned to his guests. "Go safely to your homes now. Tomorrow we will honor this traveler with a feast."

When the guests had all taken their leave and Odysseus was left alone with the king and queen, the queen spoke gently to him. "I see that you do not wear your own clothes, my friend," she said, "for those are garments that my daughter took to the washing pools this morning. You say that you have come from beyond the sea. In truth, who are you? Where is your home?"

Odysseus did not want to reveal his true identity. So he told them only of leaving the island of Calypso and escaping the terrible storm. He told them about their daughter's kindness toward him.

Satisfied with his story, the queen ordered her servants to prepare a room for Odysseus. He was soon led to his bed, where he lay down on soft purple blankets. As soon as the torches were put out, he fell into a deep, restful sleep.

❈ ❈ ❈

The next morning, palace servants set about preparing a great feast. They roasted sheep, boars, and oxen. A messenger was sent to summon the finest singer in the land, a blind minstrel.

As King Alcinous' servants made preparations for the feast, Athena walked through the streets of the city. Disguised as the king's herald, she called to every citizen: "Come, lords and princes! Come hear the stories of the stranger who has arrived at the palace of the king!"

A great crowd gathered at the palace for the feast. When King Alcinous brought Odysseus before his people, the crowd gasped. Odysseus could see great wonder in their faces. Though he was still weary from his ordeal at sea, he suspected that Athena had made him look tall and strong and given him an air of great dignity.

As the feasting began, the blind singer sat down by a pillar and cradled his harp in his arms. Soon the spirit moved him, and he began singing about famous warriors who had died in battle. He sang about the heroes of the Trojan War, about brave Achilles and King Agamemnon.

As the singer sang, Odysseus wept for his lost friends. He hid his face behind his robe, so none could see his tears. He did not want them to guess who he really was.

But later, after sports and games, Odysseus felt merry and confident. He called out to the singer: "Sing about the wooden horse that helped the Greeks win the war! If you tell the true story of the fall of Troy, I will praise your storytelling the whole world over!"

The singer began singing about a Greek king named Odysseus. He sang about how Odysseus had ordered the making of a giant wooden horse, and how he had hidden himself inside the horse with his finest warriors. He sang about how the Trojans had brought the horse inside the walls of Troy, and how the Greeks, led by Odysseus, had crept out at nightfall and laid siege to the city, and thus won the war.

As the minstrel sang, Odysseus began

to weep again. This time, he could not hide his grief. He wept uncontrollably.

King Alcinous ordered the singer to silence his harp. "Our guest has wept twice today when you sang about the Trojan War," he said. "I imagine your songs have stirred his memories." Then the king turned to Odysseus. "Sir, do not try to hide what you feel or who you are any longer," he said. "Tell us your name. Tell us about your travels and what you have seen. Did you see the fall of Troy? Did your friends perish in battle? I ask you to tell us your story."

RETURN TO ITHACA

*O*dysseus stood and faced the crowd. "Where should I begin?" he said. "I have such a long, sad tale to tell. First, I will tell you my name: I am Odysseus. My home is Ithaca, a bright and beautiful island. The island is low and the water around it can often be rough. But there is no sight more beautiful than one's own home. I have not seen my island or my family for twenty years, not since I sailed away to fight the Trojan War. . . ."

Odysseus went on to tell how the Greeks had fought for ten years in faraway Troy—and how their mighty fleet had set sail for home after winning the war. He told how a terrible storm had driven his twelve ships off course and sent them to the Land of the Lotus Eaters—and then to the cave of the hideous Cyclops monster.

Odysseus told about the horror of seeing the giant one-eyed monster eat his warriors alive—and how he had led his men in a daring escape by hiding in the fleece of the monster's rams.

Odysseus told how the Wind God had given him a bag of winds to help speed his ships home. And how, when they were within sight of Ithaca, his men had disobeyed his orders and opened the bag while he was sleeping, releasing a terrible gale that swept their ships back across the sea, far away from home.

Odysseus told how cannibal giants had murdered most of his men and sunk eleven of his twelve ships. He told how he and his crew had then sailed to the island of Circe, the enchantress, and how the beautiful witch had turned his men into pigs. He told about his journey to the mist-filled Land of the Dead, where he saw the ghosts of friends who had died, and, the saddest sight of all, the ghost of his own mother.

Odysseus told how his ship sailed past the Sirens, the strange bird-women who lured sailors to watery death with their beautiful singing. He told how his ship was forced to pass between two deadly creatures—the hideous six-headed monster, Scylla, and the whirlpool monster, Charybdis.

Odysseus told how his men had disobeyed the gods and slain the cattle of the Sun God—and how, for this offense, the gods had drowned the last of his men in a horrible storm at sea.

Odysseus told how he had then sailed alone to the island of Calypso—and how the goddess had kept him prisoner for seven long years. He told about leaving her island and clinging to a raft for twenty days and nights at sea, until he had finally crawled upon the very shores where Princess Nausicaa and her hand-maidens had found him.

At the end of his astonishing tale, Odysseus sighed with sorrow. "I want now only to return to my family," he said. "I want to go home."

All who had listened to Odysseus' story were silent with awe. At long last the king spoke: "For many years, this man has been far from his native island, and now he asks only that we help him return to his family. Tomorrow, fifty-two of our finest sailors will prepare a ship, and at sunset, we will send him on his way home."

❈   ❈   ❈

The next day, King Alcinous' servants packed a great ship with fine clothes and gifts of gold. As the sun sank low in the sky, the king's men sacrificed an ox to Zeus, almighty ruler on Mount Olympus.

"May the gods always bless your family for your great kindness and generosity," Odysseus said to the king.

The ship's sailors then laid a blanket on the deck for Odysseus. They urged him to lie on the blanket and take his rest as they set sail. In silence, Odysseus lay down on the blanket and closed his eyes.

The crew took their places. They raised their anchor and began to row. As the ship moved through the twilight, Odysseus fell asleep. After years of struggling against the ills of war, against storms and hideous monsters, he struggled no more.

The king's ship sped like a team of galloping stallions over the sea. Even falcons could not keep up with her as she moved across the purple waves.

In the hour before dawn, the ship drew close to an island harbor. Bordered by steep slopes, the harbor was free of wild winds. Its waters were calm.

The crew dropped anchor and leaped ashore. Odysseus did not stir from his slumber. The sailors wrapped the sleeping warrior in his blanket and gently carried him onto the sand. There they left him, sleeping peacefully in the shade of an olive tree. They placed his gifts near him on the sand: bronze cauldrons, golden plates, and richly woven garments. Then they returned to their ship and set sail.

After twenty long years, Odysseus of Ithaca was finally home.

THE MYSTERIOUS
SHEPHERD

When Odysseus awoke, he found himself surrounded by a mist. Through the haze, he saw strange winding paths and ghostly high cliffs. Nothing looked familiar. When he saw the gifts from the king piled near him, he fell into despair.

Why did King Alcinous order his men to sail to this place? he wondered. *Why have they abandoned me here?*

Odysseus paced up and down the beach, angry at the king for sending him to an unknown shore. When he saw a young shepherd coming toward him, he rushed to meet him.

"Greetings, friend!" Odysseus shouted through the mist. "I beg you not to fear me, but to tell me the truth—where am I? What country is this?"

"Sir, you must be a stranger to this region, if you do not know this island," said the shepherd. "It is known far and wide, from the glow of dawn to the gloom of twilight. It is a rugged place, not good for horses, but it grows grain and grapes. It receives plenty of rain, so it has good water and good grass for goats and cattle. Even those who have traveled from as far away as Troy know the island's name: it is Ithaca."

Odysseus could not believe his ears. *Surely, I would recognize my own country,* he thought. He feared the shepherd might be trying to trick him, so he quickly invented a story.

"Ah, yes, I thought so," he said, "I myself came here to Ithaca to escape punishment for killing a thief who tried to steal my treasure from the Trojan War." He pointed to the gleaming gifts on the sand.

The shepherd smiled. Then, in the wink of an eye, the young man was transformed into a tall, striking woman with gray, glinting eyes.

"Athena," breathed Odysseus.

"Odysseus, you are the world's most cunning storyteller," she said. "But still you did not know me, your guardian and protector. I have come here to help you again. I did not want others to see you, so I again shrouded you in a mist. It made your surroundings look unfamiliar to you. But never fear, this is indeed your homeland."

"Goddess, how do I know you are telling me the truth?" said Odysseus. How can I know that I have really come home?"

Athena waved her wand. "Look about you now, Odysseus," she said, "and you will see the olive trees with their long leaves. You will see the dusky cave where nymphs weave their sea-purple webs. You will see the springs that never run dry. Behold—Ithaca." As she said these words, the goddess dispersed the mist that surrounded them.

In the bright, clear air, Odysseus saw all the things the goddess had described. Joyfully he fell to his knees and kissed the ground.

"Come," said Athena, "let us hide these treasures in the cave of the nymphs. Then we will make a plan."

Together Odysseus and Athena stowed

the gold and bronze and woven clothes in the cave. Then Athena rolled a stone over the cave's entrance.

When the stone was in place and the treasures were safe, Athena and Odysseus sat on the ground beneath an olive tree. There Athena told him all about the suitors who had invaded his home.

"For several years, Penelope fought off the evil men," she said. "Finally, she promised to choose one to marry, but she never intended to do so. One of her maids reported her deceit and the suitors raged against her. Now time is running out. She mourns for you but does not give up hope."

Odysseus fought to contain his anger against those who had tormented his faithful wife. He quietly asked the goddess to help him. "Tell me what to do," he said. "Give me courage. With your help, I can fight three hundred men."

"You will fight them," said Athena. "But now, you must tell no one who you are. Suffer all you hear and see in silence, until you can take your revenge."

"But might not some of my countrymen recognize me?" said Odysseus.

"I will see to it that they do not," said Athena. "I will disguise you as an old man. I will take the hair from your head and wrinkle your flesh and dim your eyes. I will give you rags to wear, like those worn by a wretched beggar."

With these words, Athena raised her wand and passed it over Odysseus. She shriveled the smooth skin that covered his body. She took the hair from his head and the light from his eyes. She draped a ragged cloak about his shoulders and gave him a walking stick and a tattered bag.

"Be on your way now," the goddess said. "Go to the hut of your swineherd. He is a good and honest man. Stay with him while I go to Telemachus. I will bring him home from the sea where he seeks some sign that you are still alive."

"O goddess, why did you let my son drift in despair, searching for me?" asked Odysseus. "Why did you not tell him the truth?"

"Do not fear, I was with him for much of his journey," said Athena. "And even though evildoers plot to murder him, I promise you—*they* will soon die instead."

THE SWINEHERD

*O*dysseus leaned on his walking stick and trod slowly over the stony path that led away from the sea. He hobbled through the woods and over the hills to his estate.

Finally Odysseus came upon the swineherd who had long tended his hundreds of hogs. The old man sat in front of a crude stone shelter near the swine pens. He was making a pair of leather sandals. Near him lay four savage dogs that guarded the hogs.

When the dogs caught sight of Odysseus, they lunged forward, snarling and growling.

Odysseus threw down his stick and crouched on the ground. The swineherd rushed forward, shouting and throwing stones at the vicious dogs, driving them away.

"You are lucky, old man," the swineherd said to Odysseus. "In another minute, they might have killed you. Stand and come into my hut. I will give you food and wine. Then you can tell me your story—from where you have come, and what sorrows you have known."

Keeping the dogs at bay, the swineherd led Odysseus inside his simple hut. He made a seat of soft twigs, covered it with a shaggy goatskin, and invited Odysseus to sit down.

"You are kind, sir," said Odysseus. "May mighty Zeus bless you for your hospitality. May he grant your greatest wish."

"I have only one wish—that my dear master was still alive," said the swineherd. "Had he lived he would surely have given me a reward for caring tenderly for his livestock these many years. He might have given me a house, a wife, and a piece of land. But alas, my good master has been gone for twenty years. He died far away from home, returning from the war with Troy. Storm spirits destroyed his ships and all his men."

"And what of his family?" Odysseus asked softly.

"Ah, his wife waits for him in vain, while other men try to force her to marry. His mother gave up hope of his return long ago and died of grief. His father wishes to die now also—the old man no longer lives in the palace, but sleeps alone in the vine-yards. As for the son of Odysseus—the poor boy wanders the earth, looking for his father. It is tragic indeed."

The faithful swineherd sighed deeply, then stood up. "Let me feed you now, good sir," he said.

The swineherd set about preparing a meal for Odysseus. He served him meat still hot on the spit and sprinkled with barley meal. He gave him wine in a cup made from ivy wood.

As they ate and drank together, the swineherd complained to Odysseus about Penelope's suitors. "They butcher the best hogs of the farm," he said. "They slaughter the cattle and rob the storehouses and drink my master's wine. Worst of all, they torment my poor mistress night and day, demanding that she forget Odysseus and marry one of them.

Ah, but she is faithful beyond compare. She weeps for her lost husband and will not give up hope for his return."

"Do her suitors not heed her wishes?" asked Odysseus.

"Nay, these men will not leave her alone! They are cruel and without pity. I hear rumors that they now lie in wait, plotting to murder her son."

Odysseus said nothing. But in his mind, he coldly brooded upon revenge, and the seeds of the suitors' deaths were sown.

As Odysseus and the swineherd

finished their meal, a storm began to blow outside. Wind and rain pelted the roof of the small hut. The swineherd gave Odysseus more wine and asked him to tell about himself.

Odysseus lied. He said that he was born in Crete and had wandered many towns until he had come to Ithaca. "But I must tell you this," he said, "on my travels, I met a king who told me that Odysseus of Ithaca is still alive. The king said Odysseus will return home on a dark night, when the new moon is hidden. He said he might return openly or he might return in secret."

The swineherd shook his head sadly. "Do not try to raise my hopes, friend," he said. "In the past, other wanderers have passed through Ithaca with rumors about Odysseus. Each time, they have tormented his poor wife with their falsehoods. Again and again she has imagined that she might soon see her husband. Long ago, I myself believed a man who told me that my master would return in summer or in autumn. But Odysseus has never come back—and never will. I am certain that the fish have devoured him by now, and his bones lie deep in the sand of some far-away place."

As rainy darkness descended upon the stone hut, the swineherd made Odysseus a bed of sheepskins. He spread a thick cloak over him.

Then the faithful servant wrapped himself in the hide of a goat and left the hut. He went out into the dark, windy night and lay under the shelter of a rock, guarding his master's swine.

EIGHT

RETURN OF THE SON

*W*hile Odysseus had been making his way home to Ithaca, his son Telemachus had stayed on as a guest in the palace of the king and queen of Sparta.

For many days, Telemachus had wondered what to do. One night, as he tossed restlessly in bed, the goddess Athena appeared in his chambers.

Before Telemachus could speak, Athena gave him urgent advice: "Linger here no longer, Telemachus. Go home at once and protect your house. But beware—your mother's suitors plan to kill you. Right now, they wait to ambush you in the strait between Ithaca and the island of Samos."

"What should I do?" asked Telemachus.

"Sail quickly through this passage, hugging neither shore," said Athena. "The gods will send a fair wind to speed your ship on to a safe port. When you land, send your crew to town. Then go alone to your father's swineherd, the man who tends his hogs. Send him to your mother to tell her of your safe return."

Before Telemachus could ask more questions, Athena vanished from the room. Telemachus dressed hurriedly, then ran to King Menelaus' chambers. "My lord, I am sorry to take leave of you so soon, but I must set off for home immediately."

The king hated to see the son of Odysseus leave Sparta, but he consented and ordered that a chariot be prepared for him.

As Telemachus said farewell to King Menelaus and Queen Helen, a strange sight appeared in the sky. An eagle flew overhead. It clutched a great white goose in its talons.

Men and women ran across the fields. They pointed at the weird sight and cried out in amazement and fear.

"What omen is this?" someone shouted. "What can it mean?"

Queen Helen calmly answered. "The gods have revealed to my heart the meaning of this sign," she said. "The eagle stands for Odysseus. The goose stands for his home. After he has traveled far and wide, Odysseus will return home to Ithaca and take his revenge."

"May the gods make it so," said Telemachus. With that, the son of Odysseus snapped the reins of the horses and began his long journey home.

Telemachus' chariot raced across the plains of Sparta, then on to the harbor of Pylos. There Telemachus found his crew and ship waiting for him. He quickly boarded the vessel and ordered his men to raise the sail. Athena sent a fair west wind to start them on their way.

On their journey, Telemachus was careful to heed Athena's advice. He ordered his men not to sail close to either shore when they passed through the strait between Ithaca and the island of Samos.

As the black ship sped safely toward his home, Telemachus remembered more words from the goddess: *"When you land in Ithaca, send your crew to town. Then go alone to your father's swineherd, the man who tends his hogs. . . ."*

Just before they reached the port of Ithaca, Telemachus ordered his crew to strike their sail and row to land. When the ship was anchored, the crew went ashore and made a fire to cook their meat.

After all his men had eaten their fill, Telemachus spoke to them. "Now, row on to the city's port without me," he said. "I must travel alone and seek out my father's swineherd."

Once the men had cast off and the ship was on its way, Telemachus laced his fine leather sandals and picked up his mighty bronze spear. With rapid steps, he headed for the farmstead where the swineherd kept watch over the hogs.

REUNION

$\mathcal{M}$orning was breaking over the swineherd's hut. The swineherd had built a fire and was preparing breakfast for himself and Odysseus. As he poured their wine, the dogs began yelping outside.

"Your dogs sound happy—they do not snarl or growl," Odysseus said to the swineherd. "They must be greeting someone they know and trust."

Before Odysseus could say more, a young man appeared in the doorway of the hut.

The swineherd jumped up, dropping the cups of wine. He ran to the young man and tearfully kissed him. "Telemachus! My eyes' sweet light!" the old man said.

Odysseus gazed upon his son's handsome face. He was unable to move or speak. When he had last seen his beloved boy, Telemachus had been a baby. Now he was a young man with broad shoulders and a proud chest, reddish hair, and lively, bright eyes. Indeed, he looked very like his father.

Telemachus smiled at the swineherd. "You are a welcome sight to my eyes, too!" he said. "Tell me first—how is my mother? What has happened to her since I left?"

"Word came to her that you were in grave danger," said the swineherd. "She will be overjoyed to hear that you have found your way home alive.

Come inside. Eat and rest."

As Telemachus drew near the hearth, Odysseus rose silently from his seat and offered it to his son.

Telemachus shook his head. "Keep your seat, old man," he said. "Another will serve me as well."

Odysseus nodded and took his place again. His face half hidden by the hood of his cloak, he continued to gaze with wonder upon the young man.

The swineherd threw fresh logs on the fire and spread a fleece on the ground for Telemachus. Then he prepared meat from the previous night's meal and a basket of bread. He served honeyed wine in wooden cups.

When the three men had finished their meal, Telemachus spoke softly to the swineherd. "Tell me, where does your guest come from?" he said. "What ship and what crew brought him here?"

"He comes from Crete and has traveled over the world. I put him in your hands now. Offer him the hospitality of your father's house."

Telemachus shook his head sadly. "How can I take a guest into our house when it is overrun by my mother's suitors? I can only offer him gifts. I will clothe him in a cloak and tunic and give him fine sandals and a sword and send him wherever he wants to go. But for now, I will visit with him, while you hurry to my mother and tell her of my safe return."

The swineherd nodded and stood up.

"Speak to her in secret," said Telemachus. "Let no one else know I am here."

"I understand," said the swineherd. Then he took his leave of Telemachus and Odysseus and set off for the palace.

After the swineherd had left, Odysseus saw a tall, fair woman appear in the doorway of the hut. Telemachus seemed not to take notice of her, but the dogs whimpered and cowered in fear.

The woman beckoned to Odysseus. He quietly left the fire and stepped outside. He followed her to a stone wall. Facing the woman in the morning light, Odysseus saw that it was the goddess Athena.

"Odysseus, it is time to tell your son the truth," the goddess said. "Then the two of you must plan your revenge on the suitors and make your way to town together. I will follow closely behind. I am ready for a fight."

Athena touched Odysseus with her wand. Instantly, the ragged garments fell away from his body and he was clad in a fine tunic and cloak. He was taller and looked much younger. His face was bronzed; his cheeks full. He had dark hair and a dark beard.

Athena had restored Odysseus to his strongest, most vital self. Before Odysseus could speak, the goddess vanished in the morning light.

Odysseus returned to the hut. When Telemachus saw him, a look of wonder and fear came over his face. He could barely speak. "Stranger—you have changed!" he stammered. "You must be a god from Mount Olympus! Spare me harm—allow me to make a sacrifice to you!"

Odysseus spoke quietly. "I am no god, Telemachus," he said. "I am the one you have mourned for, the one for whom you have suffered great pain and injury. I am your father."

The tears that Odysseus had long held

back now streamed down his face. But Telemachus shook his head. "No—you cannot be my father—you are a demon casting a spell, or you are a god. You were an old man, and now you are young—"

"I am not an immortal," said Odysseus, "but I have been blessed by a goddess. After twenty years of wandering and torment, Athena has brought me home to Ithaca. She changed me into an old man, and now I am a young man once more. It is easy for the gods to cast a man down and then raise him up again."

Hearing these words, Telemachus

began to weep. He grabbed his father and hugged him, and the two sobbed together. Their cries were wild and piercing, like those of eagles whose young have been stolen from them. After twenty long years, father and son were finally reunited.

A PLAN FOR REVENGE

$\mathcal{S}$itting together in the swineherd's hut, Odysseus and Telemachus asked many questions of each other. "What ship brought you here, Father?" said Telemachus. "Where is your crew?"

Odysseus told how King Alcinous had sent him home with the help of the best sailors in the world. "I slept all through the voyage," he said, "only to wake and find myself alone on shore, surrounded by gold and bronze treasure. With the help of Athena, I hid everything in the cave of the nymphs. Then Athena sent me here to find you. She wishes us now to plot revenge against our enemies."

"It may be hard for us to fight all of them" said Telemachus. "We are only two, and they number nearly one hundred and twenty."

"I believe Athena will help us," said Odysseus, "as will her father, Zeus. Do you think we will then be strong enough?"

"With the help of Zeus and Athena, we will surely defeat our enemies," said Telemachus. "Tell me what we must do."

"Tomorrow at daybreak, you must go home alone," said Odysseus. "I will disguise myself as a beggar again and travel to the palace. Do not protest if the suitors abuse me when I arrive. Even if they shout names at me or throw things at me, do not speak a word in my favor."

"When will we fight them?" asked Telemachus.

"When Athena whispers to me that the time has come, I will nod to you. You must then take all the swords and spears and shields from the hall and hide them in an upstairs room."

"What will I tell the others when they ask why I am doing this?" asked Telemachus.

"Say that you are removing the weapons so they will not be harmed from the smoke of the fires. Leave weapons only for you and me—two swords, two spears, and two leather shields. And remember, my son—tell no one that you have seen me—not the swineherd, nor any of the servants, nor my old father, not even your mother. . . ."

As the day wore on, Odysseus and Telemachus made further plans. Though Odysseus had finally returned to Ithaca, he knew he could still not rest. There was one more great battle to fight—but this one he would fight with his son.

Book Six

THE FINAL BATTLE

PENELOPE

$\mathcal{P}$enelope, queen of Ithaca, wept and prayed to the gods as she waited for news of her son, Telemachus. Five weeks earlier, the young man had sailed away in search of his long-lost father, Odysseus. Shortly after his departure, Penelope had learned that her suitors were plotting to murder her son on his journey home.

For years, these wicked men had tried to take Odysseus' place. They tormented Penelope daily, invading her home and demanding that she choose one of them for a husband. But Penelope remained fiercely loyal to Odysseus. Enduring threats and humiliation, she had led the suitors on with false promises of mar-riage, then put them off again and again by refusing to choose whom to wed.

Now Penelope wept for both

Odysseus and Telemachus. As she paced in her chamber, she heard someone calling to her from the courtyard below. Penelope rushed to the window and saw the old swineherd who lived on the pig farm near the shore. The swineherd was surrounded by Penelope's servants and suitors.

"My lady, weep no more," the swineherd called to Penelope. "Your son is safe! Yesterday his ship docked at our island. He rests now at my hut."

Hearing this news, Penelope and her handmaidens wept tears of joy. But the suitors were plainly unhappy to hear that Telemachus had returned safely to Ithaca. When Penelope learned they were making a new plot to kill her son, she went downstairs to confront them. Filled with fury, she called out to Antinous, the leader of the villains.

"Antinous! Do you not remember how my husband once saved your father from an angry mob?" Penelope said. "And now you try to take Odysseus' place and murder his son! How dare you?"

Before Antinous could answer, one of

the other suitors called out from the crowd, "Do not worry, Queen Penelope! Your son has nothing to fear from us. Of course, should the gods decree that he die, there is nothing we can do."

Helpless in the face of their evil, Penelope could say no more. She returned to her chamber. She wept bitter tears for her husband and son, until finally the gray-eyed goddess, Athena, closed Penelope's eyelids and gave her the gift of sleep.

APPROACH TO THE PALACE

*T*he goddess Athena was also watching over Odysseus and Telemachus. Just two days before, Athena had helped Odysseus return to the shores of Ithaca and disguised him as a beggar.

When Odysseus had hobbled to the hut of his faithful swineherd, the old man had not recognized him. Later, when Telemachus arrived at the hut, he also did not recognize Odysseus. But when father and son were alone, Athena magically took away Odysseus' disguise. Since their joyful reunion, Odysseus and Telemachus had been making a plan to fight the suitors, whose number exceeded one hundred.

Now, huddled near an evening campfire, father and son reviewed their plot. "You will go to the palace first,"

Odysseus said. "I will follow, in my disguise as a beggar. Remember, you must not show any sign that you know me—even if someone tries to do me harm."

"And you will tell me when it is time to hide the weapons?" asked Telemachus.

"Yes," said Odysseus. "Athena has promised to help us. When she appears and gives me the sign, we will take the spears and shields from the hall and hide them in a storeroom upstairs."

Their discussion was interrupted by the return of the swineherd. Athena's magic again gave Odysseus the appearance of a lowly beggar. As the three men prepared their supper together, father and son held their plan close to their hearts.

❈　❈　❈

The next morning, at the first light of dawn, Telemachus left the swineherd's hut. His mind was filled with thoughts of the coming fight as he hurried down the rocky path toward his home.

When Telemachus reached the palace, his old nurse, Euryclea, greeted him joyfully. The other maids of the house surrounded him and embraced him.

Soon his mother appeared. She threw her arms around him and wept.

"Sweet light of my eyes!" Penelope cried. "I feared I would never see you again!"

"I have traveled far, Mother—as far as the kingdom of Sparta," said Telemachus. "King Menelaus and Queen Helen showed me great hospitality there and showered me with gifts."

"And what news do you bring of your father?" Penelope asked.

Telemachus looked at his mother sadly, remembering his promise to Odysseus to tell no one of his father's return to

Ithaca. "I know only this," he said softly. "King Menelaus said that long ago the Old Man of the Sea revealed to him that Odysseus was being held captive on the island of the goddess Calypso. He cannot leave, because he no longer has any ships to carry him home."

As Telemachus told his mother more about his journey, Odysseus was heading toward the palace. Accompanied by the swineherd, he hobbled down the rocky road in his disguise.

As they neared the palace gates, Odysseus saw an old, bony dog lying on a garbage heap. Tears came to Odysseus' eyes, for he recognized the dog as his beloved hound, Argus.

When Argus caught sight of Odysseus, he seemed to recognize his master. The old dog was so feeble he could not stand. But he joyfully wagged his tail.

It pained Odysseus that he could not go to Argus, lest he give himself away. "Why does that hound lie abandoned and uncared for?" he asked the swine-herd. "He looks as if he were once a fine animal."

"Aye, he was once the master's favorite," the swineherd said. "But with the palace in such disorder, no one thinks to care for him anymore. For years, he has waited faithfully to lay eyes upon his beloved master again. He knows not that Odysseus died long ago."

As Odysseus sadly followed the swineherd through the palace gates, the old dog closed his eyes and quietly passed into the peace and darkness of death. His greatest wish had finally come true: his master had come home.

THREE

THE BEGGAR AT THE TABLE

Leaning on his stick and covered by his ragged cloak, Odysseus stood at the threshold of the palace that had been his home twenty years before.

Soon the suitors began boisterously

invading the great hall. Invisible to the rude men, the goddess Athena appeared to Odysseus and whispered in his ear. "Go around the room and beg from each man," she said, "and you will learn who is good and who is evil."

Odysseus followed her bidding and began hobbling from man to man, begging for food.

Antinous, the leader of the suitors, took an immediate dislike to him. "What a loathsome creature you are!" he said when Odysseus approached him. "How dare you try to take our dinner?"

Odysseus looked Antinous in the eye. "And what about you, sir?" he said. "Do you not feed yourself from another man's table?"

Antinous picked up a stool and hurled it at Odysseus, striking him on the back. Odysseus took the blow silently and walked away.

Telemachus struggled against his fierce desire to defend his father, for he knew he must not reveal the beggar's true identity. But when servants told Penelope about the attack on the poor ragged man, she was furious.

"I hope the god Apollo strikes Antinous dead!" she said. "All my suitors are loathsome, but Antinous is the worst! Bring the stranger to me. Perhaps he has heard something about my husband. He seems like a man who has traveled far and seen much."

The servant hurried to relay the message to Odysseus.

"Tell your queen that I will come to her after dark," said Odysseus, "and bring her news of her husband."

While Odysseus waited for the day's end, the suitors filled the courtyard of the palace with loud singing and dancing. They quarreled and fought with one another. They shouted insults at Odysseus and threatened him.

Finally Telemachus could bear them no more. "Are you mad?" he shouted. "Have evil spirits possessed you? Leave this palace at once!"

The suitors were amazed by the young man's boldness. But, grumbling, they finally did as Telemachus commanded and took their leave.

When all the suitors had left the palace, the goddess Athena made a sign to

Odysseus. Odysseus went immediately to Telemachus. "We must prepare now for tomorrow's battle," he said. "We will remove the armor and spears from the downstairs hall. If anyone asks you why we are doing this, say that you fear they are being damaged by the heat and smoke of the household fires."

Holding a golden lamp, Athena, now invisible, led Odysseus and Telemachus through the downstairs hall. The lamp's soft glow shone upon the walls and rafters. With the help of Athena's light, father and son removed helmets, shields, and spears from the walls and carried them to an upstairs storeroom.

Then Odysseus bid good night to Telemachus. "Go to bed, my son," he said gently. "Rest for tomorrow's battle. I must go now and speak with your mother."

FOUR

THE NIGHT BEFORE
THE BATTLE

$\mathcal{D}$ark had descended and the palace was quiet. Queen Penelope sat in her ivory-and-silver chair by the fire of the great hall. Her beauty shone like that of the golden goddess, Aphrodite.

"Please bring a bench so my guest will be comfortable," she said to her maids.

A bench was brought and covered with a soft sheepskin. Then a servant bid Odysseus to come before the queen.

"Welcome, my friend," Penelope said. "Now, please tell me—who are you? Where do you come from? Where is your family?"

His face hidden by his ragged cloak, Odysseus spoke in a low voice: "Honorable wife of Odysseus, please do not ask me of my homeland or my family.

Do not force me to remember my pain and grief."

"I understand," said Penelope. "My own grief began twenty years ago when my husband left to fight the Trojan War. For many years now, men have come to court me. They have taken over our house. They tell me Odysseus is surely dead and demand that I choose one of them to marry.

"I tried to trick them for a while. I told them I would marry again when I had finished weaving a shroud for Odysseus' father. I worked on the shroud every day. But every night I unraveled my day's weaving, so the work would never be done.

"After three years of this trickery, a serving maid discovered my secret and told the suitors of my deceit. I had no choice but to finish my weaving. Now, they demand that I keep my word and choose one of them for a husband. I know not what to do. My years of grief and worry have left me with no more strength to fight these men."

Penelope sighed deeply. "There," she said. "I have told you of my family and my grief and my torment. Now, speak to me about yourself. Where are you from? I know you were not born from a rock or a tree."

Odysseus did not blink as he began to spin a tale for his wife. "I lived on the island of Crete," he said. "My grandfather was the great King Minos. I remember a time when your husband Odysseus was blown off course on his way to Troy, and he came to our island. I entertained him at the palace. He and his men stayed with us for twelve days. Then they put out to sea again."

Hearing even this simple story of her lost husband made Penelope weep. Just as the snows melted by the east wind run down the mountainside, so did the tears run down her lovely cheeks. Odysseus longed to comfort his wife, but he forced himself to remain silent.

When Penelope had spent her tears, she looked at Odysseus again. "Stranger, how shall I know if you speak the truth? If you truly have seen my husband, tell me—what did he look like? How was he clothed?"

"It has been twenty years, so my

memory of Odysseus is weak," said Odysseus. "But I will tell you how I remember him. He wore a thick purple cloak with a golden brooch. On the brooch were engraved a hound and a fawn."

Odysseus' words made Penelope weep even harder than before. "It was I who pinned that golden brooch to his purple cloak before he sailed away to war," she said through her sobs.

Odysseus could bear Penelope's tears no longer. "Please do not weep, my lady," he said. "I have heard recently that

Odysseus is alive, though all his men are dead. He will soon return home bearing great gifts. I believe he will come this very month, between the old moon and the new."

"I pray your words are true," said Penelope. "If they come to pass, you will be greatly honored."

The queen then called for her servants and told them to prepare a comfortable bed for the stranger.

"I have no need of a soft bed," Odysseus said. "I have long slept on the hard ground."

"Then at least allow my servant Euryclea to bathe you," said Penelope. "She cared for Odysseus from the day he was born until the day he sailed away to war."

Odysseus smiled and agreed to a bath. He sat silently by the firelight as Penelope took her leave and the old maidservant filled the water basin. As Euryclea began to bathe him, Odysseus remembered the scar above his knee. The scar was from a wound made by a boar's tusk when Odysseus was a young man. Before he could hide his leg, Euryclea saw the long white mark.

The old woman slowly traced her fingers over the scar. Then she looked up at Odysseus. Her eyes filled with tears. "Oh!" she whispered. "You are Odysseus!"

Odysseus grabbed Euryclea and pulled her close to him. "Woman, you must promise to tell no one who I am," he whispered fiercely, "until the gods have delivered these evil suitors into my hands."

"I promise," Euryclea whispered. "I shall be as silent as a stone."

After his bath, Penelope came to Odysseus again. "I fear the dark day has arrived," she said, "and I must finally marry one of these wretched men, or my son shall surely come to harm. So this is what I have decided to do. Long ago, my husband Odysseus could shoot a single arrow through the rings at the ends of twelve ax handles. Whoever among the suitors can string Odysseus' great bow and shoot with the same skill— he will I wed."

Odysseus nodded slowly. "I believe this is a good plan," he said. "Let the contest be held tomorrow."

Penelope smiled. "It is a great comfort to talk with you, my friend, but I must go to bed now. No mortal can go forever without sleep."

Odysseus watched Penelope climb the stairs to her chamber. Then he spread an oxhide on the floor of the hall and lay down to sleep.

But sleep would not come. Odysseus tossed restlessly, worrying about the coming fight. *I have suffered worse than this,* he thought. *I saw my own men hideously murdered by the Cyclops monster, and still*

I endured. I journeyed to the Land of the Dead. I survived storms and shipwrecks and escaped cannibal giants. . . . But no matter how he tried to reassure himself, Odysseus could not rest.

"Odysseus."

Odysseus opened his eyes. The goddess Athena was standing over him.

"Why can you not sleep?" she said. "Your wife is here, and so is your son. You are finally home."

"What you say is true," said Odysseus. "Yet I wonder if I can rid my home of these shameless suitors. They are always together in a great crowd. Even if I kill them all, surely others will come and try to avenge their deaths."

"Faithless mortal!" said the gray-eyed goddess. "Have I ever ceased to watch over you? Can we not defeat an *army* of men together? Go to sleep now. I promise you that with my help, you will prevail over your enemies."

SIGNS FROM THE GODS

*O*dysseus awoke with the first light of day. When he heard the sounds of weeping coming from Penelope's chamber, a fresh wave of worry washed over him.

He lifted his hands and prayed to the

most powerful of the gods. "O Father Zeus," he whispered, "if it is your will that I win this battle today, please send me a sign."

A moment later, thunder rumbled in the clear blue heavens overhead.

A servant was grinding corn nearby. "Thunder!" she exclaimed. "And not a cloud in sight! Lord Zeus must be sending us a sign. May this be the last day that I slave for these terrible men!"

Odysseus was glad to hear her words and glad to hear the omen from the mighty god of the skies.

As dawn spread her rosy-fingered light throughout the rest of the palace, Telemachus rose from his bed and dressed for the coming battle. He slung his sword over his shoulder and tied on his sandals. He picked up his bronze-pointed spear and left his room.

In the courtyard outside, the suitors had again gathered to discuss how they might slay the young prince. But as they plotted against the son of Odysseus, a strange sight appeared in the sky: an eagle soared overhead, gripping a dove in its talons.

"Look!" said one of the suitors. "That is surely a bad omen for us! I fear it means our plot will fail!"

The other suitors shrugged off the sign and streamed into the great hall for their morning feast. As they passed around bowls of wine, Telemachus entered the hall with Odysseus. Still disguised as a beggar, Odysseus sat on a stool near the table. Telemachus poured wine into a bowl and offered it to the ragged man.

One of the suitors laughed and stood up. "Let *me* make a contribution to the beggar's bowl!" he said. Then he hurled a cow's foot through the air at Odysseus.

Odysseus ducked, then smiled through clenched teeth at his attacker. But Telemachus whirled on the rude suitor in fury. "You may eat from our table and drink from our wine barrels!" he shouted. "But you may not abuse a stranger in this noble house!"

The suitors all burst into laughter. Then a strange wind swept through the hall, carrying a spell from the goddess Athena. The suitors could not stop their laughter. As they howled uncontrollably, their blood seemed to spatter their food.

When they were finally able to regain control of themselves, one of the men leapt to his feet. "O lost men! I have just had a terrible vision, sent by the gods! I have seen what is to happen here today! I saw the walls of this room covered with blood! And I saw the table and halls filled with ghosts—ghosts hurrying to the darkness of the Land of the Dead. . . ."

STRINGING THE BOW

After breakfast, Penelope went to the storeroom of the palace and picked up the huge bow that had once belonged to Odysseus. She carried it out to the hall and set it down before all the suitors.

"Listen to me," she said to them. "For a long time, you have overrun this house. You have drunk my husband's wine and slaughtered his livestock. You say you are only waiting for me to choose one of you to marry. Well, here is your challenge. If one of you can string the bow of Odysseus and shoot an arrow through the rings of twelve ax handles in a row, that is the man I will marry."

The suitors eagerly took up the challenge. One by one, they tried to string Odysseus' mighty bow. But even though they greased it with hot tallow and warmed it near the fire, the strong bow would not bend.

While each suitor took his turn with the bow, the old swineherd and the cowherd who had long tended Odysseus' cattle slipped out of the hall. They were sickened by the sight of their enemies handling their master's bow.

Odysseus saw the two men go and hurried after them. "Wait!" he called. "I have a question for you both. If Odysseus were to drop from the sky and appear before you today, would you fight for him? Or would you fight on the side of the suitors?"

"Oh, if only Lord Zeus would hear my prayer and lead our master home," said the cowherd, "you would quickly see my strength in fighting for him."

The swineherd nodded and uttered his own desperate prayer for Odysseus' return.

Odysseus was certain he could trust his two old servants. "You must know, then, that your prayers have been answered," he said. "I am Odysseus. And if we defeat these suitors, I will honor you both."

The two men were speechless. They could not believe that the wretched beggar standing before them was truly their master, Odysseus.

Odysseus lifted his ragged cloak, revealing the long white scar above his knee. "Remember the wound inflicted by the tusk of the boar when I was young?" he asked.

The swineherd and cowherd fell upon their long-lost master and wept.

Odysseus embraced them. "Cease your tears now, or someone will see us and tell the others," he said. "Listen carefully to my orders. When we go back inside, give me the bow, so that I may have a turn in the contest. After I have it in my hands, make certain that all the women are locked in their rooms, and throw the bar across the courtyard gate."

When Odysseus and his two loyal servants returned to the great hall, they found that none of the suitors had been able to string the bow. "Why do you not resume your contest tomorrow?" Odysseus said. "Perhaps the archer god will help one of you then. But for now, let me hold that smooth bow. I should like to see if there is any force left in my hands, or if my hard travels have taken all my strength away."

The men reacted angrily. "You fool, do not dare to touch that bow," said Antinous. "Hold your tongue, or we will throw you out to sea."

Penelope stood up. "Our guest says he comes from a noble family," she said. "Give him the bow and let him try to string it."

"Mother, return to your chamber and your weaving," said Telemachus, for he knew that a bloody battle was about to begin. "I am master of this house. I will be the one to invite our guest to string the bow."

Penelope was surprised by the sharp words of her son, but she lowered her head and returned to her chamber. As she lay on her bed and wept for Odysseus, the goddess Athena closed Penelope's eyelids and sent her into a deep slumber, sparing her from the horror of what was about to happen.

In the great hall below, the swineherd and cowherd took the mighty bow and quiver of arrows and handed them to

Odysseus. Then they hurried from the room to give orders to the maids and lock the outside gate.

Odysseus slowly examined the bow. Then he bent and strung it effortlessly, as if he were a musician stringing a harp. When he finished, he plucked the taut cord. It sang like a swallow's note.

Thunder rumbled in the sky. Odysseus smiled, for he knew the thunder was another sign from the god Zeus. As the suitors watched in stunned silence, he picked up an arrow and set it against the bow. He aimed at the row of axes,

He drew the arrow back, and let it fly.

The arrow sailed perfectly through each of the twelve ax rings.

Odysseus put down his bow and looked at Telemachus. "The stranger you welcomed into your home has not disgraced you," he said.

Telemachus nodded. The battle was about to begin.

DEATH TO THE SUITORS

*O*dysseus threw off his rags and leapt onto the stone threshold of the hall. He glared down at the suitors.

"*That* contest is over," he said. "But now there is another target for my bow.

Help me, Apollo, god of archers—"
And with those words, Odysseus took
aim at Antinous, the leader of the
suitors, and sent an arrow straight into
the villain's throat.

As Antinous fell to the floor, the
other suitors sprang from their seats.
"You will pay for this!" one shouted at
Odysseus. "The vultures will soon eat
you!" They all then rushed about in great
confusion, searching for their weapons.
But no spears or shields could be found.

"Dogs!" Odysseus shouted at them.
"I—Odysseus—have come back! You

never thought you would see me again, did you? But now your final hour has come!"

"Use the tables for shields to block his arrows!" one of the suitors shouted. "Attack him with your swords!" The man rushed at Odysseus with his sword, but Odysseus swiftly slew him with another arrow from his bow.

Another suitor ran toward Odysseus, but Telemachus hurled his spear and killed him, too. Then Telemachus hurried from the room to get arms for the swine-herd and the cowherd.

Odysseus held off the suitors with his arrows until Telemachus returned with shields and spears and gave the weapons to their two allies. Then the four men stood together against the crowd.

One of Odysseus' enemies ran up-stairs to the storeroom and found the door unlocked. He grabbed twelve spears and brought them to the others.

With the enemy now armed, it seemed impossible to Odysseus that he and his three comrades could defeat the scores of men. But suddenly the goddess Athena appeared in the hall.

"Join us in our fight!" Odysseus shouted to her.

Athena's eyes flashed. "You must prove yourselves first!" she said. Then she turned into a swallow and flew up to a roof beam to watch.

One after another, Odysseus sent his arrows streaking through the air, killing many of the suitors. Then he and his three comrades hurled their four spears at the enemy. When four of the suitors went down, Odysseus and his men pulled the spears from their bodies and hurled them again.

The suitors hurled spears, too. But Athena kept sending them astray. Finally the goddess sent a vision that struck terror into the suitors' hearts. A dark cloud appeared over the great hall. The cloud took the shape of Athena's mighty shield. The suitors knew that a vision of Athena's shield meant certain death.

Ruthlessly, Odysseus, Telemachus, and their two comrades slew man after man. Odysseus spared the life of the minstrel, for the singer sang songs sent from the gods. And he spared the herald, for he wanted him to spread the news that the men of this earth should do good and not evil.

But to all others, Odysseus showed no mercy. By the end of the battle, every suitor had been slain. Their bodies were heaped on the floor like dead fish thrown from a net onto the sand.

The god Hermes appeared in the great hall. Holding his golden wand, he led the suitors' ghosts from the palace.

Squeaking like bats, the ghosts followed Hermes over ocean waves.

They followed him past snowy rocks. They followed him beyond the sun's gate and beyond the place of dreams, until they arrived at last in the mist-shrouded Land of the Dead.

REUNION

Standing in a pool of blood, surrounded by the corpses of the suitors,
Odysseus called for the maidservant
Euryclea. When the old woman saw
the carnage, she shrieked with joy and

relief, for she knew the palace was finally free of the villains who had tormented Odysseus' family for so many years.

"Be silent," Odysseus commanded her. "It is wrong to exult over the dead."

"Let me at least go and tell Penelope," said the maid. "She has slept through the whole battle."

"No, do not wake her yet," said Odysseus. "Gather all the maids who once danced with the suitors. Order them to carry away the dead and wash the blood from the walls and floors."

Euryclea did as Odysseus commanded her. When the palace was scrubbed clean, Odysseus told her to make a fire to purify the house. Finally, as the fire sent its smoke through the halls and courtyard, Euryclea hurried upstairs to Penelope.

"Wake up!" she cried, shaking the sleeping queen. "Your beloved husband has returned! He waits for you now! Wake up!"

When Penelope opened her eyes, the old woman told her the story of the great battle and how she had found

Odysseus and Telemachus standing over the corpses of the suitors.

"Do not raise my hopes that it is truly Odysseus," said Penelope. "Surely, it is one of the immortal gods in disguise. My beloved husband is either far away on a distant island, or he is dead."

"Go and see for yourself!" urged Euryclea. "I saw the scar on his leg—from the tusk of the boar. Come with me now! He waits for you by his own fireside!"

"Old woman, you do not know the minds of the gods . . . or how they can trick us," said Penelope. "But I will go and see my son."

Penelope went downstairs. She found Odysseus sitting by the fire. His rags were covered with blood. Sweat and blood covered his dirty face and hair.

Stunned by Odysseus' savage appearance, Penelope turned away.

Telemachus rebuked her. "Mother, can you not even look at him? Is your heart so hard?"

But Odysseus was patient. He smiled and turned to Telemachus. "Let us wash ourselves and dress in fresh tunics," he said. "Then tell the minstrel to play a cheerful dance tune as if he were playing a wedding song. We must fool the neighbors, and delay the news of the slaughter from reaching the relatives of the slain. When they hear about it, they will surely seek revenge."

Odysseus left the hall, and servants bathed him and rubbed him with oil and dressed him in a clean tunic. Then the goddess Athena magically took away his beggar disguise and made him look younger and taller.

As handsome as a god, Odysseus

returned to the hearthside. He sat opposite Penelope. But still she was silent. Odysseus' transformation had made her even more mistrustful. Was this man truly a man? Or was he a god trying to deceive her?

"What a strange woman you are," said Odysseus. "After twenty years, you will not let your husband take you in his arms." When Penelope did not speak, Odysseus went on. "Well, then, I suppose I must sleep alone."

"What a strange man you are," said Penelope, "if indeed you are a man,

and not a god playing a trick on me."
Then Penelope thought of a trick of
her own. Long ago, Odysseus had built
their marriage bed from an olive
tree that grew through the floor of
their bedchamber. Only she and
Odysseus himself knew the secret
of its construction.

"I know not who you truly are,"
Penelope said, "but I will tell my maid to
prepare my own bed for you. Euryclea!"
she called, "have the servants place my
bed outside my chamber and pile it with
fleeces and sheets of linen."

Odysseus' eyes flashed with anger. "What happened to the bed I made for us long ago?" he said. "That bed could never be moved—one of its posts is the trunk of an olive tree still rooted in the ground! Has a thief cut that post and stolen our bed?"

Penelope gave a shout of joy and rushed into Odysseus' arms. "Only you would know this secret of our marriage bed!" she exclaimed tearfully. "Forgive me for doubting you!"

As his wife's arms closed tenderly about him, a deep ache rose in Odysseus' breast—the ache of a swimmer in a stormy sea who has long yearned for the sun-warmed earth. Holding Penelope in the flickering firelight of his own hearth, he wept with sweet grief.

As his mother and father embraced, Telemachus hushed the dancers and the servants. The hall was darkened, and everyone went to bed.

Odysseus and Penelope retired to their chamber, and to the bed with the post made from the olive tree. There they spent many hours of the night telling each other stories of all that had happened during Odysseus' absence.

While they talked, the goddess Athena held back the horses of Dawn—Firebright and Daybright—so the joyful couple could spend more time alone.

PEACE

*W*hen dawn finally came, Odysseus told Penelope that he must go to the country and see his father Laertes. Mad with grief, Laertes had mourned his lost son for twenty years. The old man refused even to live in the palace, preferring to sleep in rags in one of Odysseus' vineyards.

"While I am gone, lock yourselves and your maids in your rooms and speak to no one," Odysseus said to Penelope. "For I must warn you—by the end of this day, word will have spread about the death of the suitors—and their kin will surely come seeking revenge."

Odysseus then woke Telemachus, and the swineherd and cowherd, and asked them to go with him to see his father. Though it was bright morning when they set out, Athena shrouded the four men in

darkness until they came to Laertes'
vineyard far from town.

"Go to the house and prepare a meal
for us," Odysseus told the others. "I will
go into the fields and find my father."

In one of the fields of the vineyard,
Odysseus saw an old man hoeing the
ground. Bent over his hoe, the man wore
a filthy tunic and a tattered hat made of
goatskin. It grieved Odysseus to see his
father Laertes looking so weary
and ragged.

"Forgive me for disturbing you,"
Odysseus called out. "I am looking for a

friend of mine. He once stopped at my island and stayed in our house. He said he was from Ithaca and that his father was Laertes."

The old man lowered his head and wept. "That must have been my son, my unfortunate son, Odysseus," he said. "He has long been dead. Far from home, he was eaten by the fish of the sea or perhaps by wild beasts on land."

"Indeed?" said Odysseus. "It has only been a few years since I saw him. I gave him gifts and sent him on his way. I thought the omens for him were good.

We had every hope of meeting again."

Laertes nodded and his eyes filled with tears. Then the burden of his grief became too much for him. Groaning with misery, he picked up a handful of dirt and poured it over his head.

Odysseus could not bear to see his father suffer a moment longer. He rushed forward and threw his arms around the sad old man. "Father, I am your son," he said. "I have returned. And I have destroyed all those who tormented you and my wife and son."

Laertes stammered in disbelief. "Can—

can you give me proof that you are truly my son?" he asked.

"I can show you this hunting wound," said Odysseus, revealing the scar above his knee. "And I can tell you about the trees in your orchards. When I was a boy, you gave me thirteen pear trees and ten apple trees and forty fig trees."

Hearing these words, Laertes collapsed to the ground in a faint. Odysseus held his father tightly to his chest, until Laertes opened his eyes again. A smile of joy spread over the old man's face—then a look of fear.

"I am afraid that soon the families of the slain suitors will come seeking revenge," said Laertes.

"Do not worry about them now," said Odysseus. "Come, let us go to the farmhouse and have a meal together with your grandson, Telemachus."

Odysseus helped his father to the house, where a great feast awaited them. There the old man bathed and dressed in a fine cloak. The goddess Athena gave youthful energy to his frail limbs and made him taller and stronger.

In the midst of their celebration, an angry shout came from outside. Armed men had indeed come seeking revenge for the death of the suitors.

Odysseus, his father, and his son quickly pulled on armor and went outside. Laertes hurled his spear through the air and killed one of the men. Odysseus and Telemachus held up their swords and prepared to meet their enemy.

At that moment, Athena appeared. "Hold back!" she cried. "Stop, before another drop of blood is shed!"

Odysseus' foes turned pale at the sight of the great goddess. They dropped their weapons and fled in terror. Odysseus let out a savage battle cry. He swooped like an eagle after them.

But mighty Zeus threw a thunderbolt to earth. Seeing this sign, Athena called Odysseus back. "Cease fighting, Odysseus, before you anger the gods!" she cried. "All fighting must end! Let there be peace from now on!"

Odysseus was relieved to hear these words. He gladly gave up the pursuit of his enemies. He knew that with the blessing of the gods, all his battles were over—battles against Trojan warriors, against monsters of the deep, against terrible storms, and against enemies at home. Odysseus had survived each and every one, and was finally reunited with his beloved family.

From that day on, and for many years to come, peace reigned on the island of Ithaca, and the gods looked favorably upon Odysseus, his wife, and his son.

ABOUT HOMER AND THE ODYSSEY

Long ago, the ancient Greeks believed that the world was ruled by a number of powerful gods and goddesses. Stories about the gods and goddesses are called the Greek myths. The myths were probably first told as a way to explain things in nature—such as weather, volcanoes, and constellations. They were also recited as entertainment.

The first written record of the Greek myths comes from a blind poet named Homer. Homer lived almost three thousand years ago. Many believe that Homer was the author of the world's two most famous epic poems: the *Iliad* and the *Odyssey*. The *Iliad* is the story of the Trojan War. The *Odyssey* tells about the long journey of Odysseus, king of an island called Ithaca. The tale concerns Odysseus' adventures on his way home from the Trojan War.

To tell his tales, Homer seems to have drawn upon a combination of his own imagination and Greek myths that had been passed down by word of mouth. A bit of actual history may have also gone into Homer's stories; there is archaeological evidence to suggest that the story of the Trojan War was based on a war fought about five hundred years before Homer's time.

Over the centuries, Homer's *Odyssey* has greatly influenced the literature of the Western world.

GODS AND GODDESSES OF ANCIENT GREECE

*T*he most powerful of all the Greek gods and goddesses was Zeus, the thunder god. Zeus ruled the heavens and the mortal world from a misty mountaintop known as Mount Olympus. The main Greek gods and goddesses were all relatives of Zeus. His brother Poseidon was ruler of the seas, and his brother Hades was ruler of the underworld. His wife Hera was queen of the gods and goddesses. Among his many children were the gods Apollo, Mars, and Hermes, and the goddesses Aphrodite, Athena, and Artemis.

The gods and goddesses of Mount Olympus not only inhabited their mountaintop but also visited the earth, involving themselves in the daily activities of mortals such as Odysseus.

THE MAIN GODS AND GODDESSES AND PRONUNCIATION OF THEIR NAMES

Zeus (zyoos), king of the gods, god of thunder

Poseidon (poh-SY-don), brother of Zeus, god of seas and rivers

Hades (HAY-deez), brother of Zeus, king of the Land of the Dead

Hera (HEE-ra), wife of Zeus, queen of the gods and goddesses

Hestia (HES-tee-ah), sister of Zeus, goddess of the hearth

Athena (ah-THEE-nah), daughter of Zeus, goddess of wisdom and war, arts and crafts

Demeter (dee-MEE-tur), goddess of crops and the harvest, mother of Persephone

Aphrodite (ah-froh-DY-tee), daughter of Zeus, goddess of love and beauty

Artemis (AR-tem-is), daughter of Zeus, goddess of the hunt

Ares (AIR-eez), son of Zeus, god of war

Apollo (ah-POL-oh), god of the sun, music, and poetry

Hermes (HUR-meez), son of Zeus, messenger god, a trickster

Hephaestus (heh-FEES-tus), son of Hera, god of the forge

Persephone (pur-SEF-oh-nee), daughter of Zeus, wife of Hades and queen of the Land of the Dead

Dionysus (dy-oh-NY-sus), god of wine and madness

PRONUNCIATION GUIDE TO OTHER PROPER NAMES

Achilles (ah-KIL-ees)

Aeolus (EE-oh-lus)

Agamemnon (ag-ah-MEM-non)

Alcinous (al-SIN-oh-us)

Antinous (an-TIN-oh-us)

Argus (AR-guss)

Asteris (ahss-TER-iss)

Calypso (cah-LIP-soh)

Charybdis (kah-RIB-dis)

Circe (SIR-see)

Crete (KREET)

Cyclops (SY-klops)

Euryclea (yoor-ih-KLAY-ah)

Ino (EYE-noh)

Ithaca (ITH-ah-kah)

Laertes (LAY-er-teez)

Medon (MEE-don)

Menelaus (men-eh-LAY-us)

Mentor (MEN-tor)

Minos (MEE-nohss)

Nausicaa (now-SIK-eye-ah)

Nestor (NES-tor)

Odysseus (oh-DIS-yoos)

Penelope (pen-EL-oh-pee)

Polyphemus (pah-li-FEE-mus)

Pylos (PY-lohs)

Samos (SAH-moss)

Scheria (SKER-ee-ah)

Scylla (SIL-ah)

Sparta (SPAR-tah)

Taphos (TA-fohss)

Telemachus (Tel-EM-ah-kus)

Trojans (TROH-junz)

A NOTE ON THE SOURCES

The story of the Odyssey was originally written down in the ancient Greek language. Since that time there have been countless translations of Homer's story into other languages. I consulted a number of English translations, including those written by Alexander Pope, Samuel Butler, Andrew Lang, W.H.D. Rouse, Edith Hamilton, Robert Fitzgerald, Allen Mandelbaum, Robert Fagles, and E.V. Rieu.

Homer's *Odyssey* is divided into twenty-four books. Book Four, *The Gray-Eyed Goddess*, was derived from books one through five, and part of book fifteen, of Homer's *Odyssey*. Book Five, *Return to Ithaca*, was derived from books 6, 7, 8, 13, 14, 15, 16 (with brief references to the events that take place in books 9-12). The sixth volume, *The Final Battle*, was derived from books 16 through 24 (with brief references to the events that took place in books 9-12).

ABOUT THE AUTHOR

MARY POPE OSBORNE is the author of the best-selling Magic Tree House series. She has also written many acclaimed historical novels and retellings of myths and folk-tales, including *Kate and the Beanstalk* and *New York's Bravest*. She lives with her husband in New York City and Connecticut.

Zeus

Hera

Artemis

Hephaestus

Apollo

Ares

Athena

GODS *and* GODDESSES *of* ANCIENT GREECE

Hermes

Dionysus

Aphrodite

Hestia

Demeter

Persephone

Poseidon

Hades